Wakening

DEREK JOHNS has been a ⟨…⟩ r and now works as a literary ⟨…⟩ London. His first novel ⟨…⟩uring Billy Palmer was *Wintering*.

From the reviews of *Wakening*:

'An elegant, accurate and heartfelt novel.' *Scotland on Sunday*

'Derek Johns has a wonderful economy of style and can transport the reader with a very few deft phrases and the result is a charming study of a young man's salad days with the promise of more adventures to come.' *Refresh*

'His evocation of the lost world of 1960s publishing is extraordinarily vivid.' *The Times*

'An endearing account of the long pilgrimage to adulthood.' *TLS*

'*Wakening* is written in a deceptively simple style, unvarnished and unadorned, but always resonating with a true sense of time, place and experience.' *Sunday Business Post*

'The novel's sense of place is strong and authentic.' *Time Out*

'Johns' style is delightfully simple, which makes for an enticing coming-of-age novel.' The Tablet

'A nostalgic and atmospheric coming-of-age novel.' People's Friend

'Wannabe bohemians harking back to the glory years of flares and free love will feel a pang of jealousy reading this story.' Big Issue

'Johns is a master of [simple observation], capturing the flavour of the times with tenderness and precision. Wakening is one of those coming-of-age novels with the quiet force of memoir: moments of awkwardness captured in aching detail; snatches of dialogue with freshness and authenticity. The best thing in the book is the evocation of 1960s Bloomsbury [and] one of the most attractive things about the character is his underlying integrity. Yes, he wants to drop out, live a bit, see the world. But he is also looking back over his shoulder to the family he has left behind in Somerset. His scratchy relationship with his father is beautifully rendered. Johns is vivid storyteller, with his finger on the pulse of the quiet passions that animate ordinary lives.' Sunday Telegraph

'An account of the shattering yet liberating effect that wanderlust can have on a young life, [and] Johns has written a worthy successor to the Palmer family tale that he began with Wintering.' Financial Times

Wakening

Derek Johns

Portobello
BOOKS

Published by Portobello Books Ltd 2008
This paperback edition published 2009

Portobello Books Ltd
Twelve Addison Avenue
Holland Park
London W 11 4QR, UK

A CIP catalogue record is available from the British Library

9 8 7 6 5 4 3 2 1

ISBN 978 1 84627 136 6

www.portobellobooks.com

Designed by Richard Marston
Typeset in Joanna by Avon DataSet Ltd, Bidford on Avon, Warwickshire B50 4JH
Printed and bound in Great Britain by CPI Bookmarque, Croydon

'To wake the soul by tender strokes of art'

Pope, Prologue to Addison's *Cato*

One

Billy sat in Goody's café poring over the map of Morocco. It was a map of wonders, of mountains and gorges and dunes, of places with beautiful names like Zagora and Taroudant. There were green palm trees, and everywhere the symbol that indicated a kasbah. What exactly was a kasbah? Billy wondered. He had been reading Walter Harris's *Morocco That Was*, an account of his time there at the turn of the century. Was it possible to travel in that way now, without a classical education and a private income? At Bristol he had been immersed in Robert Byron and Peter Fleming when he should have been reading the Brontës and Mrs Gaskell. Byron's 'stony, black lustred' Persia and Fleming's news from Tartary had captured his imagination. Now it was Morocco that had caught him in its spell, a place that was not so far away but which nonetheless seemed utterly remote. And he had fastened upon it all of his hopes for the future. He must go to Morocco to discover who he was.

He looked out of the window at the bleak February day. In a while he would be home, and his parents would learn that he had dropped out. There would be a scene, he knew very well. But he had determined on this course some time ago, and it was too late to turn back now. The conversation with his professor had settled it for him. 'You have a sentimental response to literature, Palmer,' he had said. 'You lack rigour.' Billy had held his tongue, but that had been the moment when he knew he wanted no further part of it. He would listen to no homilies about the right way to read: he would read as he wished, just as he would live as he wished.

What he wished for now was to be able to go straight to Marrakesh, but that would require money, and he must work for a while first. He looked down again at the map. From Marrakesh you had to cross the Atlas Mountains and keep heading south for the dunes. And then there was nothing but sand until Timbuktu.

———

He watched his father's cigarette smoke as it coiled towards the ceiling. There was something mesmerizing about it.

'I'm going anyway,' he said.

Jim brushed a piece of lint from the lapel of his suit and looked at Margaret for help.

'But you would have had all the time in the world to travel after your degree,' she said.

'I can't wait that long, Mum. I'm bored to death in Bristol. And what good is an English degree anyway?'

'You'd have found that out if you'd got one,' said Jim. He stared at Billy in dismay. 'What are you going to do with your life anyway? Become a gypsy?'

'I'll work in a bookshop in London for a while. Save some

money. Then when I come back from Morocco, we'll see.'

Jim stood up and went into the kitchen. He returned carrying a bottle of whisky and a single glass. 'You're doing exactly the sort of thing I did,' he said. 'I thought sons were supposed to learn from their fathers' mistakes.'

'Let's not get onto the subject of your mistakes,' said Margaret.

'Cheers,' Jim said ironically. 'Here's to my eldest son's brilliant career.' He drained the glass in one gulp. 'You were going to be a teacher,' he said. 'You were going to make something of yourself.'

Billy heard the familiar tones of self-pity in his father's voice. Whose life was it they were talking about, Jim's or his?

'I was never going to be a teacher, Dad,' he replied. 'I only said that because I had no idea at all what I wanted to do.'

'Well you fooled me.' Jim stalked out of the room again. Billy and his mother looked at one another for a few moments without speaking.

'You know,' said Margaret at last, 'for once your father is right. Life without a degree may be much less fulfilling than you think.'

He crossed the room and sat beside her on the sofa.

'You don't understand,' he said. 'I've never been out of the country. There's a whole world out there.'

His mother sighed, and then leaned over to kiss him on the cheek. 'Perhaps I understand better than you think,' she said. 'I've always regretted the fact that I've never been abroad. I used to daydream about going to France.'

'You can go to France. I don't know why Dad hasn't taken you. He's doing well enough these days.'

'We've talked about it. But I'm thinking of when your father and I were your age. We simply didn't have any choices to make then.'

'There was a war on,' intoned Billy, repeating a phrase he must have heard a thousand times. He gazed at her earnestly. 'Well, this is my war,' he said. 'This is my adventure. I'll suffocate if I don't go now.'

'Then you must go.'

He raised himself up. 'I'm going for a walk with Tom,' he said. 'I'll come back to say goodbye.'

Sarah was hovering in the hallway, taking an unnatural interest in the newspaper.

'We've got to talk,' she whispered.

Billy followed her up the stairs.

'What's going on?' she said as she closed her bedroom door behind them.

'I've dropped out.'

'Wow! What are you going to do?'

'Work in a bookshop for a while, probably, to earn some money. Then go to Morocco. But it's not what I'm going to do, it's what I'm going to be.'

'What's that?'

'A free spirit.'

'Great. That's what I'm going to be too.'

'You already are.'

'I am, aren't I?'

He looked at her fondly. She was always getting into trouble these days, hanging around with boys, smoking and drinking. She drove their father wild with anger sometimes, and Billy was forever coming to her defence.

'Lee's joining a band in London,' she said, 'and he's asked me to stay with him in the Easter holidays. We can get together.'

'Of course. But let me get settled first.'

He went into Tom's room and hauled him off the floor, where he was playing with his Scalextric.

'Let's go outside,' he said. 'I've got something to tell you.'

They walked up Priory Road, Tom holding his hand. He seemed very young for eight; but then he was the youngest by far, and loved to distraction by the rest of the family. Billy had hated leaving him when he went to Bristol, and hated even more the idea of leaving him again now.

They passed the Regal. 'Dad's spelled the name of that film wrong,' said Tom.

Billy looked up at the marquee. 'It's called *Bullitt*,' he said. 'It doesn't have any bullets in it. Or maybe it does. It has a car chase that's meant to be very exciting.'

He halted for a moment to look at the cinema, the place where he had spent so many Saturdays helping out while he was at school. It was an ugly block of a building with a few art deco touches. For his father it represented respectability after the lost years in the wake of his bankruptcy. Billy heard Jim's words echoing in his mind, about sons learning from their fathers' mistakes. What had he learned from his own father? His impulse was invariably to do precisely the opposite of what Jim expected.

In Market Place the stalls were set out on the cobblestones. How quaint Wells seemed now. It was as though the clocks had stopped fifty years ago, five hundred even. They sat on a bench overlooking the moat of the Bishop's Palace and watched the swans glide by.

'I'm going away,' said Billy.

'But you went away before.'

'This is different. I'm going to travel.'

'Where will you go?'

'To a place called Morocco.'

'Where's that?'

'In Africa. Well, at the top of Africa. There's a city called Marrakesh that has a big square with snake charmers and story-tellers. And oranges. And camels.'

'I'd like to ride on a camel.' Tom looked up at him quizzically. 'But why are you going there?'

'Why?' Billy fell silent for a few moments. 'Well, I've always wanted to travel. And there's something about the desert. It's going as far as you can go. And it's empty and silent.'

Tom's face assumed a baffled expression.

'I'm not explaining it very well, am I?' said Billy.

'Not really.'

'OK. When I was a kid, not much older than you, I wanted to climb Glastonbury Tor. For a long time Dad wouldn't let me, and it seemed impossibly difficult. Ever since then I've wanted to do something impossible. Going to the desert is that thing.'

He ruffled Tom's hair. Was this really why he wanted to go to Morocco? It was only as he uttered the words that this justification had occurred to him. He looked up at the towers of the cathedral, and quite suddenly the boldness he had been feeling drained out of him.

———

He stood by the side of the Bath road, his thumb pointing resolutely east. Having hitch-hiked often enough before, he knew not to expect quick results. But he had left it late today, and darkness would come in a couple of hours. His departure had been delayed by one thing after another, as though neither he nor his family could quite believe he was going. It was very cold, and he fastened the top button of his combat jacket. After a stream of cars had coursed by, eventually a flat-bed lorry pulled over. Billy ran towards it, only to find that the cab already contained three men.

'On the back,' said the driver.

He slung his duffel bag onto the platform, and sat leaning against a roughly bundled tarpaulin. There was no guard-rail, and he set his hands firmly to either side of him so as to stay in place as the lorry negotiated the winding road. The countryside unfolded backwards, making this familiar road seem new. Good, he thought: I want everything to be new.

They dropped him off at the junction with the motorway. As he stood on the slip-road he could sense the light fading. No one would pick him up in the dark. He shivered in the icy air. The expressions on the faces of the drivers as they accelerated past him were impassive, grim even. But eventually a Ford Zephyr drew up, the driver leaning across to push open the door.

'London?' said Billy.

'Hop in.'

He was about fifty, balding and with a jowly face. 'Where in London?' he said.

'I don't really know.'

'You don't know?'

'Where are you going?'

'Home, me. Stepney.'

'Where's that?'

'The East End. But you don't want to go there, I can tell you.'

Billy looked out of the window as the car gathered pace. He hadn't thought much about where he would stay. It began to dawn on him just how impulsive his decision had really been: he hadn't planned anything at all.

'What do you do in Stepney?' he asked.

'I work for Ford's, in Dagenham. That's what gives me this smart car.'

'Right.'

'And what are you going to do?'

'I want to work in a bookshop.'

'Oh well, in that case Foyles is your best bet.'

'I suppose so. It's not my idea of a bookshop, somehow.'

'But it's big. There'll be more chance of a vacancy.'

Their conversation faltered very soon, and as darkness fell, Billy took to wondering what he might expect. He hadn't been to London for a couple of years now, and he had never felt very easy there. It was simply the place you went to when you dropped out. But now it began to loom in his imagination, this vast city that he knew so little about.

They drove on, the traffic becoming steadily heavier as they approached the city. It was night by the time they arrived, and Oxford Street was deserted. The driver pulled over, and pointed down a road to his right.

'It's just a few yards,' he said. 'But you'll need to find somewhere to stay.'

'Yes. Where?'

'The university's that way. There have to be rooms. Look in a newsagent's window.'

Billy thanked him, and walked down Charing Cross Road. Immediately Foyles came into view, a large building with red lettering running along the length of its frontage. 'The World's Largest Bookshop', it read. Gazing into its windows at the books on display, he began to feel that his quest was taking shape, becoming real. Foyles gave him something solid he could attach his hopes to. It was where he would begin.

He turned back in the direction of the university, looking for a newsagent, but found none. Unsure where to go, he kept on walking, quickly losing any sense of direction. The city was very quiet; he must simply be in the wrong part of it. Coming to a large square, he sat down on a bench and gazed up at the phosphorescent orange of the sky. The reality of his situation oppressed him now: here he was in a place where he knew almost no one, had nowhere to stay, and had very little money. A wave of exhaustion washed over him, and suddenly he knew that this bench was as far as he was going. He laid out his sleeping bag, climbed inside it fully clothed, and within minutes he was asleep.

He awoke feeling stiff and cold, and went in search of breakfast. Russell Square had been his shelter for the night, he discovered, and by the Tube station he found a greasy spoon that was open. He ate a vast breakfast, and afterwards found a newsagent with a board full of handwritten signs. 'Room to let in Store Street,' he read. 'Three pounds a week. Share of bathroom.' He noted the address, and asked a passer-by to direct him. Across the road from a café called Lino's he found the door. It was ages before anyone answered the bell.

'Yes?' said a woman. Her face was indistinct, and Billy's first impression was of a halo of grey hair.

'It's about the room,' said Billy.

'Come in, then,' she said.

He stepped inside the door and into a narrow hallway.

'You're a student,' said the woman, as if stating an incontrovertible truth.

'Yes,' said Billy. The moment he uttered this he realized that it was no longer true. But if he wasn't a student, what was he?

'Follow me.'

She was quite tall, and wore an oriental robe. Her movements were graceful and unhurried, and it seemed to Billy that their ascent of the stairs was interminable. Eventually they came to a door, which she opened tentatively.

'I'm not going to make any excuses for it,' she said. 'It *is* only three pounds a week, after all.'

It was very small, containing a bed, a chair and a chest of drawers. There was a sink at the far end and a single-ring stove. The meter bore a large sign that read 'Shillings only'. It was a lonely room. But then what could he expect? Billy pressed his hand down onto the mattress and turned to the landlady.

'I'll take it,' he said.

She showed him the bathroom, took his first week's rent, and gave him a key. He locked the door and lay down on the bed, gazing at the unshaded light bulb above his head. At least I'm in London, he thought; at least I've begun.

———————

He went out later for a bite to eat, and spent the evening in his room, reading. The next morning he went for a walk. Shunning the places where the tourists went, he headed east, and found himself exploring Clerkenwell and Blackfriars. He came upon the river, and leaned over the stone balustrade. The pleasure boats cut swathes across the river, the sunlight flaring on the water. He walked back along the embankment, and then got lost in Covent Garden. The market was silent now, the arcades empty. On this Sunday morning London was somnolent. As he stood wondering which street to take, he felt lost in more ways than one. Since the moment he had left home he had been assailed by a sense that he had cut himself adrift. He chose a direction at random, and it led him into a maze of backstreets. It was ages before he found his way to the boarding house, and by then he felt utterly dispirited.

He left it until mid-morning the next day before going to Foyles. Charing Cross Road was bustling now, London had come alive. The boy behind the counter directed him to an office where a woman took down his details.

'Miss Foyle interviews all candidates personally,' she said. 'She is available tomorrow afternoon at three.'

When he returned, he found Christina Foyle's office at the very top of the store. She sat stonily behind her desk, reading Billy's application form.

'How old are you?' she asked.

'Nineteen. I'll be twenty in May.'

'That's a very bad age.' She looked at him over her glasses. 'Why aren't you at university still?'

'I... I left. It wasn't what I wanted.'

'It seems to me that young people want far too much these

days.' She fussed with her glasses case for a few moments. 'And what makes you think working in a bookshop is what you want?'

Billy shrugged his shoulders. 'I just love books,' he said.

'We have a rule about staff reading books: not on the company's time.'

'I don't mean...'

She snapped the case shut. 'We don't have any vacancies at the moment,' she said. 'We'll keep your name on file.'

Out in the street, Billy felt dazed by this conversation. She hadn't given him a chance to explain himself. But then, how *was* he going to explain himself? He had better get his story straight. He walked past the other bookshops nearby, and decided he needed some time before he tried anywhere else. He wandered aimlessly among the crowds, beginning to feel overwhelmed. The city was frenetic now, so different from the place he had arrived in a couple of days ago. Everyone except him seemed to have something to do and somewhere to go. He turned back towards the boarding house, and the sanctuary of his room. And then, lying idly on his bed, he wished he had someone to talk to.

The next morning he tried Better Books, which was just across the road from Foyles. The man he spoke to shook his head regretfully. 'We've recently been taken over,' he said. 'I'll be letting people go, not taking them on.'

He walked down the street, trying one bookshop after another, and being turned away from every one. All his hopes seemed absurd now, his assumption that finding a job would be easy, that he would be seized upon as the sort of person anyone would be grateful to hire. It began to rain, a steady drizzle, and by the time Billy reached the boarding house he was soaked. He spent a sleepless night, wondering how long this search would take and how long he could endure it.

The following day he tried the antiquarian bookshops in Museum Street. Looking into one of the shop-fronts at the first editions of Joyce and Eliot, it dawned on him that this was the place he and his father had come to a few months after they had moved to Glastonbury. Jim had borrowed a car and they had picked up some packages from a shady-looking man in Wells and delivered them to a shop in this very street. Billy looked up and down and saw a sign that read 'Bernard Smith: Antiquarian & Second-hand Bookseller'. That was the place. The books had been stolen, as Billy had sensed at the time and later understood. His father had said he was doing a favour for a friend, but Billy had known even then that he was doing it for money. He stood in front of the window of Smith's shop and considered going in, but then thought better of it.

He had no luck with any of the other shops in the street. And then, in the late afternoon, he came across a bookshop he hadn't seen before, hidden away just a few doors up from Foyles. He peered through the window into a narrow space in which display tables nudged against the bookshelves. It was with a sense of trepidation that he entered Collet's and asked to see the manager.

He sat behind his typewriter, a man with a jutting jaw and a pipe clamped in his mouth. His moustache was a motley of grey and yellow.

'You've dropped out,' he said, a smile of self-satisfaction creasing his face. 'I can always tell.'

'Well... yes.'

'This place is full of drop-outs,' he said. 'Drop-outs, Maoists, anarcho-syndicalists – we've got the lot here.'

'I want to work with books.'

'Of course you do.' He rattled the stem of his pipe against his teeth and swept ash from his bright-red cardigan. 'Fiction?'

'Yes, fiction mostly.'

'Someone's leaving the fiction department at the end of the week. Going to Cuba, so he reckons.'

'I didn't think you could get into Cuba without being invited.'

'You can't,' said the manager, and he burst into a high-pitched giggle. When he had regained his composure he said, 'Andrew Wilson. Pleased to have you with us.'

They shook hands, and Billy realized that he had a job. Wilson led him to the fiction department, and introduced him to the woman who ran it.

'Beverley Hoskins, Billy Palmer,' he said. 'He's starting next Monday, taking over from Kevin.'

She was probably about thirty, and very plump. She smiled and said, 'I look forward to working with you.'

'Me too,' said Billy enthusiastically.

The days until he started at Collet's were hard to get through. He passed the shop often enough, staring at the window displays and wishing himself already there. He tramped the streets, crisscrossing the city, setting out his coordinates. London was vast, inexhaustible.

When he wasn't out walking, he sat by the gas fire in his room, reading Durrell's *Justine*. The fire hissed, and in its glowing reticulations he conjured images of Alexandria, its 'thousand dust-tormented streets'. How odd it was, he thought, that he could be so easily transported by a book to one great city when another lay on his doorstep and yet seemed nonetheless remote.

Eventually the following Monday came around. At half past nine Billy reported to Andrew Wilson, who told him to find Beverley. 'You'll have to do the donkey work,' he said. 'She's not the most agile.' Wondering how important agility might be in bookselling, he went off in search of her.

She stood behind the counter, going through stock cards. Her dark-brown woollen dress went all the way to the floor, seeming both to conceal and accentuate her girth. She smiled her shy smile, and set Billy to work opening boxes of books. They bore the black and orange Penguin imprint, and there were lots of them.

'Just put them on the shelves,' she said, 'moving books up

where you need to. Put as many face-out as you can: it's nicer that way.'

Billy began to work, checking off the titles against the despatch note. He was surprised to find how many authors he had never heard of who, judging from the numbers of their books, must be quite popular. It was hard work stacking the shelves, and he began to see what Wilson meant by agility. In the middle of the morning Beverley brought him a cup of coffee, and then suggested she introduce him to the staff. There were three other assistants on the ground floor, who looked after the hardbacks, the crime books, the science fiction and the poetry, and downstairs three more. The basement had an air of studiousness, its signs indicating politics, economics, sociology and history. The other assistants were either very young or very old, and they seemed friendly enough. He said hello to them in turn. And then he saw a ghost.

He was the whitest person Billy had ever seen. Behind thick glasses his eyes blinked continually, as though he were staring at the sun. They were a dull pink colour, and quite unsettling.

'Peter Burns,' he said. 'No relation to Robbie.' He glanced away as he shook Billy's hand, as though at someone else, and then looked back. His eyes seemed fathomless. Throughout the rest of the morning the image of this strange creature kept recurring to Billy, and he found himself glancing down the stairs now and then so as to try to catch sight of him.

He finished stacking the Penguins, and Beverley asked him to mind the counter for a while. The customers came and went, generally handing over their books without a word. Then a military-looking man stepped towards him.

'You don't seem to have Pole's *The Valley of Bones*,' he said.

'Let me see,' said Billy. 'Pole?'

'Yes. Anthony Pole.'

He went to the shelves, but could see no books by anyone called Pole. Returning to the counter he looked at the stock cards, and drew a blank there too.

'No, we haven't,' he said. 'Perhaps I could order it for you.'

'No matter,' said the man. 'I'll go to Foyles. You really ought to have all the Poles, you know.'

Beverley returned a few minutes later, and Billy decided he had better report this encounter. As he was describing it, she put her hand to her mouth.

'Oh, Billy,' she said. 'Follow me.'

They went to the shelves, and Beverley took up a book and handed it to him. *The Kindly Ones*, Billy read, by Anthony Powell.

'It's pronounced "Pole",' she said, her eyes glistening with mirth. 'He's writing a series of novels called *A Dance to the Music of Time*. He's famous.'

Billy's cheeks flushed. 'Of course,' he said. 'I just didn't know how the name was pronounced. I'll go after him and explain.'

'Don't be silly. We haven't got *The Valley of Bones* anyway – it's reprinting.'

'I'm sorry.'

Beverley laid a hand on his arm. 'Don't be,' she said. 'This is your first day, after all. You'll learn soon enough.'

———————

'Come and have tea,' said the landlady, Mrs Allingham. 'I always invite my young men to tea. And they always seem to be young men, not young ladies: girls prefer sharing flats.'

He had seen her glide about the house, always in her oriental silks, and was struck by her elegance and composure. But nothing had prepared him for the sight of her rooms. From the drabness of the hallway he stepped into a tropical den. Everything was bamboo and lacquer and porcelain. A brilliantly coloured folding screen took up one corner, its peacock's eye staring balefully out. This was another world entirely.

Mrs Allingham invited him to sit in a carved-wood chair, and poured the tea. Billy looked into his cup to see a faintly green liquid, half a dozen large leaves resting on the bottom. She didn't offer him milk.

'You'll be wondering where all this comes from, of course,' she said.

'Yes.'

'Malaya. Or Malaysia as they call it now.'

'You lived there?'

'For most of my life.' She sipped her tea, holding the cup in both hands. 'My husband was a rubber planter.'

'What's it like?'

'Oh, I loved it. The jungle isn't anything like what most

people imagine. It's clean and bright. And everything is very simple, at least for an Englishwoman with servants and not very much to do.'

'Why did you come back?'

'My husband died. Men don't last long in the tropics. We had to come home during the war, of course; and then we returned in forty-six. But it wasn't the same – one could see that independence was coming.'

She laid down her cup and brushed back a strand of long grey hair. Her fine-boned face was a tracery of lines, around her eyes and mouth, across her cheeks and forehead.

'But I've invited you to tea to find out all about *you*,' she said, 'not talk about myself.'

'About me?'

'Of course.' Her eyes sparkled mischievously. 'You told me a little white lie, didn't you?'

'Yes. How did you know I'm not a student any more?'

'You don't keep student hours.'

'No, I suppose I don't.'

'So what *do* you do?'

'I work in a bookshop, Collet's. I've just started.'

'Well, that's a very fine thing to do. And you'll write a novel, won't you?'

'No. I'm not a writer. I want to travel. But I need to spend a few months in London first.'

She poured more tea, the pithy leaves circling in Billy's cup. 'And what about your family?'

Billy had been hoping he could forget about his family for a while. In the dusky light of Mrs Allingham's sitting room he found it hard to summon anything he wanted to say.

'It's just a family,' he said. 'You know.'

'There's no such thing as "just a family". What does your father do?'

Billy sighed, and took another sip of tea. 'He owns a cinema in Wells, in Somerset,' he said.

'Is that interesting?'

'I used to work there on Saturdays. It depends on what film is showing.'

'And your mother?'

'My mother...' Billy paused for a moment. What did he want to say about her? 'My mother is a saint.'

'And by that you mean that your father is a sinner?'

Billy fell silent, not sure how to reply, and an awkwardness came over them. Finally he said, 'I don't suppose my father is any more of a sinner than anyone else. But he went bankrupt when I was ten, and we had a difficult time for a few years before he was able to get a decent job again.'

'And your mother held things together.'

'Yes. It's what mothers do, isn't it?'

———

By the end of his first week, Billy had grasped the basic elements of his job. And indeed they were very basic, involving far more physical work than he had imagined. Beverley dealt with the publishers' reps, while Billy lugged books from the stockroom and filled the shelves. He spent at least some time behind the counter, and enjoyed displaying the knowledge he already possessed about books and writers. But there was so much he didn't know, so much he hadn't read.

On the Friday he bumped into Peter Burns as he was leaving the shop to get some lunch.

'Fancy a bite?' said Peter.

They walked under an archway that led them into Soho. In Old Compton Street they entered a café called 2i's. 'Home of the Stars', read the sign. Sitting down at a plastic-covered table, they shouted at one another over the hubbub of conversation and the screech of the tall silver coffee machine.

'Have you ever seen any stars in here?' said Billy.

'They used to have music downstairs. I think the word "stars" is used rather loosely.'

Peter was studying the menu in a way that wholly obscured his face, holding it about three inches away. He squinted, and turned the card this way and that. But when the waitress arrived he said simply, 'The usual,' and to Billy, 'spaghetti bolognese.'

Billy looked around the steamy room. The other diners were mostly young, but smart, the men's hair tidy and the women in miniskirts and tight jumpers. It seemed an odd sort of place for Peter to come to.

'So how's it going?' asked Peter.

Billy set out his knife and fork and smoothed down the napkin. 'Fine,' he said. 'I'm enjoying it.'

'Beverley's all right. And Wilson is just about tolerable.' Peter blew his nose loudly and then began excavating it with his handkerchief.

'How long have you worked there?'

'Two years. I went there because of its traditions, but they're all gone now.'

'What traditions?'

'Radical ones. The original Collet's was on the site of a place they called the "bomb shop", because of its connections with anarchists. Then in the thirties the owner started bringing in communist literature from Russia.'

'But Wilson told me you were all radicals even now.'

'Well, I am. And maybe Philip Walters, though I suspect he's a backslider.'

'So what are your politics?'

'Oh, I'm a Marxist,' he said airily.

'Are you a member of the Party?'

'Of course not. The CP in this country is a bunch of lackeys.'

For so mild-mannered a person, Peter was very declamatory in his speech. Billy had stayed out of politics at Bristol. But there was something about this strange young man that he felt himself drawn to.

Their spaghetti arrived, and they tucked into it hungrily.

'Surely Marxism has failed,' said Billy after a few moments.

Peter wiped his nose with the sleeve of his shirt. 'It's not

Marxism that's failed,' he said, 'it's Russian-style communism.'

'Aren't they the same thing?'

'Not at all. Marxism has never been put into practice, it's never been given a chance.'

'So what *have* they got in Russia?'

Peter tapped his fork on the side of his plate. 'They've got a corrupt form of the dictatorship of the proletariat,' he said. 'Only it's the dictatorship of Brezhnev and his gang.'

'Wasn't that bound to happen? Doesn't communism go against the grain of human nature?'

Peter snorted. 'Human nature!' he exclaimed. 'That's precisely the point. Human nature isn't some fixed, immutable thing – it's socially and historically conditioned.'

'Is it?'

'Of course it is. The reason communism hasn't worked in Russia is that people are still alienated, from their work and from the things their work creates. But Marx foresaw all this. He knew there would have to be an intermediate stage, a period of socialism, before true communism can establish itself.'

Billy chewed on his spaghetti. He had heard this kind of speechifying before, and didn't believe a word of it. He looked across the room. A blonde girl wearing a long velvet coat and a feather boa sat down in a booth.

'Why do you come here?' he said.

Peter smiled broadly. 'I like to keep my eye on the bourgeoisie.'

They sat for a while gazing at the girls. It seemed very

clear to Billy what Peter meant by 'the bourgeoisie', and he wondered whether his own yearnings were as plain to see as his companion's.

After a while Peter said, 'What about you? What are you interested in?'

Billy looked down at his empty plate, and then out of the window. 'I want to see the world,' he said.

'That sounds pretty corny, if you don't mind my saying so.'

'I suppose it does. But I don't know how else to put it.'

'So you're going to do the Englishman abroad thing, are you, and look loftily upon the natives?'

Billy smiled. Talking to Peter was nothing if not bracing. 'I'm going to be a traveller,' he said. 'I'm going to go to Morocco and disappear into it.'

'You mean not come back?'

'No, I mean become invisible, and try to absorb things.'

Peter pushed his glasses up the bridge of his nose. 'Well I don't want to go anywhere,' he said. 'Right here will do me. I just want *here* to be as different as possible.'

―――――

The weekends were long and lonely, and Billy filled them as best he could with reading and walking. He had no money for the pleasures of the city, his bookshop wage taken up by rent and food. It was already clear that saving for Morocco was going to be difficult. And knowing almost no one in London, he was wholly dependent on the people he met in the shop.

Billy sensed a friendship forming with Peter, but he seemed preoccupied with his political activities. He spoke of his selling the *New Left Review* on street corners as a kind of crusade.

There was in fact one person Billy knew in London, but he hadn't seen him since he was Tom's age. Len Haskell was his mother's brother, and he had cut off Billy's family after Jim had gone bankrupt. Billy had never understood why he had reacted in this way. His father had owned a Jaguar showroom that went bust, and for several years afterwards he had worked in a clothes outfitters in Wells. With the cinema he had got himself back on his feet. But Len had never relented. When Billy called home one day his mother gave him Len's number, urging him to phone and to try to mend things. And eventually, with nothing better to do, he did phone, and arranged to go to the house on a Sunday morning.

He took a bus, which lurched through Camden Town and up the hill to South End Green, where he found the little terraced house on Constantine Road. The net curtains in the bay window were drawn back, and a middle-aged man peered out. When he opened the door, Billy set eyes on someone quite other than the slim, dark uncle he had known as a boy. He was portly, his hair turning to grey, his complexion florid. As he led Billy into the sitting room the soles of his leather slippers rapped on the floor.

'You're tall, like your dad,' Len said as he lowered himself into an armchair, gesturing to Billy to take the sofa.

'I suppose so.' Billy looked around the room, at the heavy

furniture and flock wallpaper. Len's wife had died many years ago, and Billy had never known her. The room they sat in seemed careworn and neglected.

'And how is he treating that sister of mine these days?'

'Oh, well, I think.'

Len pulled on the wings of his waistcoat. It was shiny and gold, and lent an odd splash of colour to the scene.

'Better than he has done, I hope.'

'He's doing his best. You know he owns a cinema now.'

'I heard.'

'He was the manager for a few years, and then he borrowed some money from the bank and bought it from the owner.'

'Always very good at tapping people for a loan, your dad. Sherry?'

'Thank you.'

Len lifted himself from the chair and padded into the kitchen. While he was gone, Billy inspected the framed photographs on the mantelpiece. They seemed very old, studio shots of Len and his wife Betty. He stepped over to the window and gazed out into the overgrown garden. A dog was barking furiously somewhere nearby, and it jangled Billy's nerves. He hadn't expected to enjoy this visit; but nor had he expected his uncle to seem quite so stern.

'So what are you doing in London?' said Len when he returned.

'I'm working in a bookshop.'

'Interesting?'

'Yes. I love being surrounded by books.'

'Like your mother.' He poured out the sherry, spilling some of it onto the tray. 'But she never had the time to read, not properly. Should have married someone who could read too.'

Billy knew he must change the subject. 'How about your work?' he asked.

Len harrumphed into his sherry. 'My work is the same as it ever was, and as it ever will be.'

'Insurance.'

Len nodded gravely. 'Insurance,' he replied. 'Against a rainy day.'

Billy sat wondering what to say next. Before he could muster anything, however, his uncle spoke again.

'You could stay here,' he said.

Billy looked at him in surprise. The expression on Len's face had softened, and what Billy had taken to be bitterness had turned to something more like melancholy.

'Thank you,' he murmured. 'I... The boarding house is very close to the shop.'

Len shrugged his shoulders. 'Just a thought,' he said. 'The spare room's quite large. Take a look at it before you go if you like.'

When, twenty minutes later, Billy left the house, he realized that he hadn't seen the room after all, that his uncle's offer had completely gone out of his mind, and that Len hadn't mentioned it again. He looked back at the bay window, remembering the dreariness of the room behind the curtains, and knew he would not be seeing his uncle again, not for a while at least. He thought of his mother, of the disappointment she would feel. Why hadn't she tried to mend things with Len herself? he wondered. His father had sworn he would never speak to him again, and, as was so often the case, it was his will that had prevailed. Perhaps he should return after all, and try to persuade Len to visit Wells. Perhaps he shouldn't always accept his father's ideas about their family.

In South End Green he sat in a corner café eating a sandwich and wondering what to do next. He had heard that Hampstead Heath was a good place to walk, the nearest thing to the countryside that London had to offer. Finding the road that led up to Parliament Hill, he came out onto a blustery knoll that gave him a broad view of the city. Kites flew in circles, children screaming at their fathers to keep them in the air. London was laid out before him, and Billy could see for the first time the way the landmarks stood in relation to each other. The Centre Point office block, which he passed every day on his way to work, loomed incongruously above the surrounding buildings; the Post Office tower seemed from here to be like a toy rocket; and the dome of St Paul's winked at him in the sunlight, a light that seemed at last to hold some promise of spring.

He walked between the ponds, and found himself in Highgate. Soon he saw the wrought-iron gates of a cemetery, and he wandered inside. There was something about the place that suited his mood, the doleful expressions of the stone angels and the tombstones that bore heavy phrases such as 'fell asleep' and 'passed away'. And then he came upon a tomb quite unlike anything else, a solid block of stone with a great shaggy head above it. 'Workers of all lands unite,' said the inscription, and below, 'The philosophers have only interpreted the world in different ways; the point is to change it'. Billy looked up again at the brooding visage of Marx, and thought of Peter. The point is to change it. But how?

At coffee break the next morning he told Peter about his explorations.

'That's Orwell's café in South End Green,' he replied.

'I don't think it was called that.'

'No, no,' he said impatiently. 'It's where he wrote *Keep the Aspidistra Flying*. Terrible book. He just wasn't a novelist.'

Peter took out his handkerchief and blew his nose loudly. He was always doing this, thought Billy, even though he seemed not to have a cold.

'What about *Animal Farm* and *Nineteen Eighty-four*?'

'Manifestos,' said Peter, 'not novels.'

'You can read them that way, I suppose. But don't you think they hold up as stories?'

'Maybe.' Peter stuck the handkerchief back in his pocket. 'We had a joker in here recently looking for Orwell's restaurant guide.'

'Restaurant guide?'

'Yes. *Dining Out In Paris And London*.' Peter smirked, and then said, 'So you're a fan of Orwell's?'

'Yes.'

'Then it seems to me you've got the makings of a revolutionary consciousness. There's an International Socialists' meeting in support of Dubček and the reformers this week. Want to come?'

'OK,' he said. 'Thank you.'

A few days later they went to the meeting at Conway Hall, going through a pillared foyer lined with wooden pews into a crowded room. Eventually they found spaces at a table at the back in which to sit.

There was almost no one over twenty-five. Most of them were young men, their uniforms of jeans and baggy sweaters worn with pride. There were a few young women, and Billy couldn't help but notice the way Peter's eyes rested on them. An older man banged his shoe on a table and called for silence.

'Welcome to the meeting,' he said, 'whether you're a member of the IS or not. We're here to express our solidarity with Alexander Dubček and his supporters. For those of you who've had your heads in the sand lately, after the atrocious events of last autumn, Novotný has had to concede the party leadership to Dubček, and the chance of reform is within their grasp. Last week the editors of *Literarni Listi* were reinstated. And Dubček is holed up in his rooms reading.'

A cheer went up from many in the audience.

'Yes, Czechoslovakia has a leader who can read!' went on the speaker. 'Who has the humility to believe that there are things he can learn if he is to lead his country into a brave future. A man who knows that the idea that socialism and democracy can't coexist is a bourgeois myth, that the crimes of Stalinism have nothing to do with true socialism.'

He was warming to his theme. 'Now Dubček must purge the party,' he went on, 'must clear out the apparatchiks. There must be a new political order. Once democratic socialism has been established in Czechoslovakia it can sweep the Eastern bloc. Then the fascists in America and the West will no longer be able to say that the project has failed. It hasn't even begun!'

Peter shouted, 'Let the revolution come!' Billy looked across at him. His whiteness, usually so pallid, seemed now to shine. He was clearly galvanized by the moment.

Other speakers came and went, and there were interventions from the floor. But everyone was in essential agreement, and the atmosphere was friendly and relaxed. The meeting broke up, and they stepped out into the night.

'So, what did you think?' said Peter as they crossed the square.

'It was interesting.'

'Only "interesting"?'

Billy paused, and then said, 'I don't know what it accomplished. Will your meeting here in London change anything on the streets of Prague?'

'It's about solidarity, about showing the world that we're watching.'

'Does Brezhnev care who's watching?'

'He will,' said Peter with an air of determination. 'Look, if you want to see what action can do, the next Grosvenor Square demo is the Saturday after next. Fancy taking part?'

'Like the one last autumn, marching on the American Embassy?'

'Yes. Except this time we're going to occupy it.'

'I'm going to a talk at the Royal Geographical Society that day. I'll meet you afterwards if you like.'

Peter gave him a withering stare. 'You're not with us, are you?' he said.

'No, I don't think I am.'

———

Andrew Wilson yanked the steering wheel of the minivan to the right, and they swung into Gower Mews. From the moment Billy had slid into the passenger seat, Wilson had been doing a fine impression of a complete madman, racing around the streets of London, cutting up cyclists and other drivers with relish. His pipe stuck out at a jaunty angle, and there was a gleam in his eye.

'Let's say hello to Pat and George,' he said.

A sign on a door at the end of the mews read 'William Heinemann, Trade Counter'. They entered to find two middle-aged men, one of them typing with two fingers and the other calling out the titles and quantities of books.

'Afternoon, gentlemen,' said Wilson.

The men replied without breaking off from their tasks. It was clear to Billy that some sort of ritual was being enacted. Wilson handed one of them an order form.

'How's business, then, Andrew?' the man asked.

'Could be worse.'

'Could be better too, I expect.'

'Could be better. Especially if it'd stop raining.'

The man returned with about a dozen books cradled in his arms. 'You know what you lot are always saying about the weather, don't you?' he said. 'If it's raining customers stay at home, and if the sun's shining they go out and do something more exciting than buying books.'

'It's an unalterable law of bookselling,' said Wilson.

He signed for the books, and they made their way back to the van and along the Euston Road. Billy was glad of this invitation to get away from the shop for a couple of hours and tour the publishers' trade counters, and glad too of the opportunity to get to know Wilson.

'Have you always been at Collet's?' he asked.

'No, I used to work at Foyles. Well, I grew up at Foyles, learned my trade there. But that was when old William was alive.'

'I had an interview with Christina before I came to you.'

'Battle-axe,' said Wilson.

Billy looked out of the window at the traffic halted all around. 'Why are there so many bookshops in the Charing Cross Road?' he asked.

Wilson adjusted the pipe in his mouth. 'I don't know,' he said. 'It's like districts in medieval towns, isn't it? Booksellers attract each other. A couple of hundred years ago they were all near St Paul's.'

'What was bookselling like in those days, when you started?'

'Not much different.' Wilson engaged first gear, and the minivan sprang forward a few yards before coming to an abrupt stop once again. 'Better Books tried to change it, but it didn't stick. They decided it would be a good idea to have silver bookshelves, so you couldn't see them. Bloody eyesore, it was.'

'That's not much of a change.'

'Oh, they did more than that. They had poetry readings and events and things. They even had tables with typewriters on them, so that writers could bash out their stuff.'

'That's a good idea.'

Wilson jammed the gear-stick forward once again. 'Writers should stay out of bookshops,' he said.

They stopped at the Collins trade counter in York Way, and then headed north. The rain lashed the windscreen, the wipers scraping back and forth. They pulled up outside a circular building and ascended an outside staircase to the first floor.

'The Old Piano Factory,' said Wilson. 'Duckworth's.'

The place was a litter of desks, chairs, papers and books. No one took any notice of them, continuing to go about their work with an air of nonchalance that Billy sensed was at least partly for show. Behind the desks were row upon row of book stacks. Wilson strode towards them, and was quickly lost from Billy's sight. An owlish-looking man in heavy black spectacles glanced up at him.

'New boy?' he said.

Billy nodded.

'You'd better go and see what Wilson's up to back there. Whenever he comes I have to go in afterwards and measure the dust on the books.'

'The dust?'

'The best form of stock control I know.' He thrust out his hand. 'My name's Colin Haycraft.'

'Billy Palmer.' He looked around him. 'This is what I always imagined a publishing house would look like.'

'Well this is about the only one that does, nowadays. The big publishers don't clutter their offices with anything so unsightly as books.'

Wilson returned, and dumped a pile of books onto one of the desks. He nodded at Haycraft. 'You're in danger of having to reprint this one,' he said, holding up a Greek history.

'No fear,' replied Haycraft. 'I'm sure demand will dwindle nicely soon.'

Back in the minivan, Billy sat thinking about these people he now found himself among. He had always thought of books as the repository of all that was worth preserving, and booksellers as their custodians. But there was something a little odd about Wilson and the others. There they were, surrounded by all the knowledge of the world, and yet in their different ways they seemed unworldly. But books could take you only so far. This was why he was going to Morocco, why he was no longer content just to read about it. This was why he was different from them.

Two

The man at the podium in the Royal Geographical Society was gaunt and ill-looking. Gavin Maxwell was famous for his island off the coast of Skye, and the otters he had raised there. But today he was talking about the Glaoui, a Berber tribe who until a few years ago had practically ruled Morocco. Maxwell coughed frequently, and gulped water from a tall glass. His voice was thin and reedy, his tones aristocratic. Lords of the Atlas his book was called, and he told an extraordinary story, of two brothers who had parlayed their control of the main pass over the Atlas Mountains into control of the entire country, and under the very noses of the French.

The slides projected behind Maxwell showed a fortress in the mountains, palaces in Marrakesh and Fez, and warriors on horseback dressed in colourful robes, their rifles pointing at the sky. It seemed scarcely possible that the last of the Glaoui brothers had died, and Morocco had secured its independence, only twelve years before.

Billy looked around the auditorium and up at the gallery. This was the shrine of British exploration, made famous by Livingstone and Stanley, by Scott and Shackleton. Billy looked back at Maxwell. He had apparently been a spy, a racing driver, a poet and a painter. As he spoke now, Billy could see the colours and hear the sounds of Africa in his words. He longed to be there. And then he remembered that he had less than ten pounds to his name.

After the lecture he tried to seek out Maxwell. There were so many things he wanted to ask him, about what life was like in Marrakesh, about how far you could go into the desert. But Maxwell had been spirited away to a private room, and a woman told Billy he would not be able to follow.

Disheartened, he strolled across Hyde Park and towards the café in Marylebone where Peter had said he would meet him after the march. Since the evening at Conway Hall they had kept off the subject of politics. A bond was forming between them, it was clear, but not one that grew out of shared interests.

He found the café, and ordered a cup of coffee. He had no idea when to expect Peter, especially given his ambition to occupy the embassy. In the event it was past six when he appeared, and when he did so he made an appalling sight. As he reeled across the room, Billy saw that there was blood matting his hair and trickling down his forehead.

Billy leaped up from his chair and led Peter to the table. 'What happened?' he asked.

'Bastards charged us,' replied Peter, sitting down heavily. His glasses were askew, and he took them off and put his hand to his face. He stared at the blood on his fingertips with an expression of utter perplexity.

'The police?'

'Yes. On horseback. One of them hit me with his truncheon. It was a riot. There were people lying on the ground all over the place.'

His words came in a halting sort of way, and he took deep breaths as he spoke. Billy looked again at the wound on the side of his head.

'This is terrible,' he said. 'You need to have that looked at straight away. Let's get a bus to my place.' He knew little about first aid, and could think only of Mrs Allingham. She would know what to do.

They boarded a bus, facing down the stares of the other passengers. Peter was clearly in great pain. He sat looking into space, groaning now and then and feeling the wound with his fingertips.

'Leave it alone,' said Billy.

Mrs Allingham ushered them into her rooms, and immediately set about boiling water and tearing strips from an old sheet.

'You foolish boy,' she muttered. 'There are better ways of making your point.'

She tended Peter's head, washing it thoroughly and winding bandage after bandage around it. 'You must see a doctor soon,' she said. 'Head wounds can be very dangerous.'

Peter was beginning to register his surroundings now, his eyes taking in the scene. 'Have I been transported to Vietnam?' he said with a puzzled smile.

'No,' said Mrs Allingham. 'You're exactly where you ought to be. And your next stop must be a doctor's surgery.'

'I'm all right.'

'No, you're not. Now, I'll make a cup of tea, and then Billy will take you to see my doctor. I'll give you his address and phone number. You may have to call him out at this time on a weekend, though.'

After dutifully drinking Mrs Allingham's tea, they went up to Billy's room. Peter sat down in the armchair. 'I don't need a doctor,' he said. 'I'll be fine.'

'Are you sure?'

'Yes.' He looked up at Billy, his eyes glinting. 'I did it,' he said. 'I showed those bastards what for!'

Sarah had said she would meet him in Portobello Road, which turned out to be very long. Eventually he found her at a stall, wearing a new coat.

'How do I look?' she said, twirling around.

'You look great.' He kissed her on the cheek. 'How could you afford it?'

'Dad gave me some money for the trip. I'll be almost broke now, but I couldn't not buy it, could I?'

'No, you couldn't not buy it.'

It was good to see her, to see a familiar face after all this time. Since they were children she had always been able to draw him out of himself, into the here and now.

'Where are you staying?' he asked.

'In Earls Court. Lee's band has a crash-pad there. I'll be here for two weeks. I'm so excited!'

It was Saturday morning, and the place was thronged with people enjoying the spring sunshine. They weaved their way down the hill, past places selling clothes and fruit and vegetables. Sarah was clearly entranced by it. The other shoppers were mostly young, their clothes brightly coloured, their hair flowing freely. This was the very heart of things, thought Billy, this was where it was at.

'You should buy something too,' said Sarah. 'You've had that awful jacket since you were at school.'

Billy looked down at himself, at the combat jacket and jeans he had worn every day since he had arrived in London. 'I'm not much interested in clothes,' he said.

'Well, I think you should get interested. How are you going to find a girlfriend looking like that?'

Billy felt suddenly wounded by his sister's words. He hadn't had a girlfriend in a long time, and by now this seemed unnatural. No matter how often he told himself there were other things he wanted, this absence from his life was something he felt keenly.

'Let's have a drink,' he said, and they stepped into a crowded pub. He struggled towards the bar, while Sarah found a corner seat and claimed it.

'So, what are you going to get up to while you're here?' he asked when they were settled.

'I'm going to hang out with Lee and the band. They're throwing a party for my birthday next weekend. You must come.'

Billy hadn't met Lee. He was surprised that his parents had permitted Sarah to stay with him, and wondered what sort of story she had told them.

'What's the band called?' he asked.

'The Tricksters. They're influenced by the Stones.'

'How are they doing?'

'They've only just formed. They've done some gigs in Bath and Bristol, and they've got their London debut soon.'

'What does Lee play?'

'Lead guitar. He's great.'

She sipped her orange juice and sat back against the worn velvet of the seat. They gazed out across the smoke-filled room, and then Billy said, 'How are things at home?'

Sarah looked down into her glass. 'They're OK,' she said quietly.

'And what does that mean?' He looked at her intently. 'Come on, how are things really?'

She hesitated, and then said, 'Dad's been impossible lately.'

'Why?'

'I don't know. I think he's… I think he's got problems at the cinema.'

Billy sighed deeply. 'You mean it's not doing very well.'

She nodded. 'And he's driving Mum crazy.'

His thoughts turned to his mother, to the woman who had 'held things together' after the bankruptcy. She had gone through so much then, so much hardship and uncertainty. Surely she would never have to do so again?

'How is she?' he asked.

'All right, otherwise. Wants to go back into the acting, now that Tom's a bit older.'

'Good. She needs to get out of the house.'

'But let's not talk about home. How are you?'

Billy shrugged his shoulders. 'OK,' he said. 'The bookshop's sort of interesting. But I don't want to be in London, I want to be in Marrakesh. London's too much, in a way, there's too much to take in.'

'I think you're mad. London's wonderful. I wish I could live here.'

'You will one day.'

'One day, yes. When I'm too old to enjoy it.'

Billy smiled, and looked across the room. Was life something that was always lived in the next place? Perhaps he should forget about Morocco and make the best of things where he was. Perhaps he should try to make a go of book-selling. But even as he had this thought he knew it was out of the question.

'I've made a friend, anyway,' he said.

'Who's that?'

'His name's Peter Burns. He's an albino and a Marxist.'

'Cool.'

'He was in the Grosvenor Square demo and got hit on the head by a policeman's truncheon.'

'Everyone's talking about Grosvenor Square. Was he really there?'

'Yes. He asked me to go with him.'

'And of course you didn't.'

'Why do you say that?'

Sarah's face assumed an expression of mild reproach, but she said nothing.

'OK,' said Billy. 'But I'm going to do something of my own. Just you wait and see.'

———

Billy and Peter had agreed they could afford to go to 2i's for lunch twice a week. They usually sat at a table at the back, studying the other diners.

'What sort of stuff do you read?' said Peter one day.

'Oh, a lot of fiction. The last good book I read was *Catch-22*.'

Peter sniffed. 'American,' he said.

'Not everything American is bad, you know. Anyway, what's *Catch-22* if not an anti-war book?'

'Can't say I've bothered to read it.'

Their lasagne arrived. 'So what are *you* reading at the moment?' said Billy.

'*One-Dimensional Man*, by Herbert Marcuse.'

'Oh, him.'

'You're not a fan, I take it?'

'I've barely read him. His books seem impenetrable.'

'He says we're living one-dimensional lives, and that our

capacity for independent thought is withering away.' As he spoke, Peter placed his elbows firmly on the table and steepled his fingers. 'It's a sort of update on Marx's false consciousness,' he continued. 'Though I don't think Marcuse is a true Marxist, not an orthodox one anyway.'

'Ideas have to develop, don't they?' said Billy. 'Things change.'

'I suppose so.' The bandage on Peter's head was lopsided, and he raised a hand to straighten it. 'I thought *Eros and Civilization* was pretty good.'

'What was that about?'

'Oh, the fact that people should be able to screw around without the state interfering.'

Billy looked across the café, at the young men and women who talked earnestly to one another amid the steam and the shouts of the waiters. 'Isn't that happening anyway?' he said.

Peter's expression turned gloomy. 'I suppose so,' he said. 'Don't ask me.'

Billy looked at his friend, and then back across the room. 'Do you have a girlfriend?' he asked tentatively.

'What do you think?'

'I don't think anything.'

'What sort of girl is going to go out with me?'

'What do you mean?'

Peter laid down his fork with an air of finality. 'I'm a freak, Billy,' he said.

'Of course you're not a freak.'

'Oh no? Look at me. I'm a weirdo. At least, that's what they called me at school.'

'School doesn't count. I'm sure no one calls you a weirdo now.'

'They don't *call* me one.'

Billy looked away again, strangely disturbed by this turn in the conversation. Then he found himself blurting out the words, 'I've never slept with a girl.'

'Well, that makes two of us.'

He looked once again at Peter, who was gazing wistfully at a table of girls nearby, and felt a powerful urge to talk about himself. His virginity was by now a matter of great embarrassment to him. He would be twenty in a few weeks' time, and furthermore his sister, who was barely seventeen, was surely sleeping with her boyfriend. But now was not the moment for such confidences.

'We need to meet some girls,' he said lightly.

'And how do we do that?'

'My sister's having a party next week. You're invited.'

'How come?'

'Because I've invited you.'

———

The band's crash-pad was in Earls Court, a basement flat just around the corner from the Tube station. Billy and Peter had a drink in a pub nearby beforehand, loosening themselves up. By the time they arrived the place was crowded, the air already sweetened by dope. Sarah hugged Billy excitedly.

He had told her he was bringing Peter, and she was very solicitous, introducing him to her friends as the hero of Grosvenor Square. And then she took Billy by the hand and led him into the kitchen.

'This is Lee,' she said shyly.

He was a willowy figure, with long eyelashes above piercing blue eyes, and sculpted lips.

'Heard a lot about you,' he said.

'How are things going with the band?'

Lee grinned. 'Well enough,' he said. 'It takes time.'

Another boy joined them, brandishing a beer bottle.

'This is Julian,' said Lee, 'our singer.'

Julian thrust out his hand in a curious gesture, pointing it at the floor. 'Julian Saunders,' he said. He looked Billy up and down. 'Anyone ever call you Bill?'

'Billy's my name.'

'Billy the Kid.'

With that Julian turned on his heel and went over to kiss a girl. He wrapped his arms around her neck, almost throttling her with the beer bottle.

'Don't mind him,' said Lee. 'It's just an act.'

Cream's 'Strange Brew' echoed around the room, spacey and dizzy-making. Many people were just lounging around listening to it. Peter was talking to a girl who sat in a corner. As Billy approached them she said, 'I am I and you are not I.'

'I can't fault your reasoning,' said Peter, smiling.

'You are very white,' she said, as though noticing him now for the first time.

'And you are very high.'

'High and white,' she said, and she began to chant the words repeatedly, 'high and white.' Then she giggled, and burped. 'I like you,' she said. Peter took this as an invitation to sit next to her. As he did so, for an instant his easy smile vanished, to be replaced by a scowl of pain. Billy hesitated for a few moments, but Peter's smile returned as quickly as it had left. He went looking for someone else to talk to.

'This is Art, our drummer,' said Lee, introducing him to a boy wearing overalls and unfashionably short hair.

'Sarah tells me you're influenced by the Stones,' said Billy.

'Are we? Fucked if I know.'

A little later the fourth member of the band, whom Billy had not yet met, pulled out an acoustic guitar and called for the record player to be turned off. He began singing 'Like a Rolling Stone'. People started joining in, and Billy did so too. He heard the strains of Peter's voice above the others', and watched him wailing out the words. And then suddenly Peter let out a cry, and held his head in his hands. Billy rushed across the room to his side.

'What is it?' he said.

Peter couldn't speak, but simply groaned.

'Get up,' said Billy. 'I'm taking you home.'

Peter got unsteadily to his feet. The room had fallen silent now, and people looked on aghast. It was clear that he was in a bad way. He leaned on Billy for support, and they crossed to the door. Billy kissed Sarah hurriedly, and they stepped out into the night.

'You must see a doctor,' he said. 'This is crazy.'

'I hate doctors,' said Peter through gritted teeth. 'I spent my entire childhood being prodded by them.'

They took the Tube to Angel, and then walked to the flat Peter shared with two others from the bookshop. Once they were inside, Peter's pain seemed to ease.

'It was like nothing I've ever known,' he said, wiping snot from his nose. 'Like another blow to the head.' He sat down, but immediately stood again and ran to the bathroom. Billy heard the sounds of vomiting. He turned to Philip, one of Peter's flatmates. 'He's got to be made to see a doctor,' he said.

Philip made a despairing gesture with the palms of his hands. 'Ever tried telling him something he doesn't want to hear?'

Peter emerged from the bathroom. 'I'm going to bed,' he said. 'Thanks, Billy. See you on Monday.'

Out on the street the air was almost balmy, the first night Billy could remember since he arrived in London that wasn't cold. He walked westwards, towards King's Cross and home. The image of a policeman's truncheon crashing down on Peter's head kept coming into his mind. Sarah had described Peter as the hero of Grosvenor Square. Was he a hero, or was he a dreamer who had discovered the hard way that the world could be unkind?

———

As the weeks passed he became more settled in the bookshop. In the course of placing thousands of books on the shelves he had become familiar with them, at least with their authors and titles and blurbs. He knew how to deal with customers, and Beverley gave him more and more responsibility. And in his own reading he was striking out too. One day, when he and Beverley were talking about writers, she said, 'You've never really told me what you like to read.'

'I suppose not.'

'I think it's about time you and I got to know each other better. Shall we have a drink after work?'

They went to the French House pub and sat in a niche at the back, surrounded by photographs of actors and boxers. The place was quiet at half-past five, but steadily filled up with what Billy thought of as the bohemian element of Soho. He liked to imagine glamorous lives for these people, in the theatre, in films, in photography and design. He knew that in all likelihood they were bit-part players, but nonetheless they were a lot more colourful than the sort of people he knew. A fat man asked in a fruity voice for a vodka and tonic, and then surveyed the room as though to invite applause.

'Coming up, George,' said the girl behind the bar.

'And a nice chaser of *you*,' said the man, his eyes sparkling merrily.

'So,' said Beverley, placing her wineglass on the table, 'what do you read?'

'Oh, the usual. I think my own reading's only just beginning.

At school and university you read what you're told to. The classics, the stuff they think is good for you.'

'They're classics for a reason.'

'You sound like my mother.'

'God forbid I should sound like anyone's mother!'

'I don't mean...' Billy's voice trailed off. There *was* something motherly about her, and it wasn't just that she was so large. 'I don't mean you're as *old* as my mother, or anything.'

'Good,' she said. 'I'm actually quite young, you know.'

They fell silent, and after a few moments Billy said, 'I haven't really answered your question, have I, about what I read.'

'No.'

He paused, trying to summon the right words.

'I think I'm looking to books to tell me how to live, who to be. Does that make any sense?'

'Of course.'

'Since their authors have presumably lived more than I have.' He looked across the room. 'There's this character in Bellow's *Seize the Day* who's obviously got it all wrong...'

'Tommy Wilhelm.'

'Yes. He's absurd, and childish. Yet by the end of the book he's come to some sort of awareness of this, he's grown. I'd like to think that I grew with him.'

'In the end you need more than books to tell you how to live, though.'

'I know. I've been reading a lot of travel books, and all they do is make me want to get away.'

She caressed her glass. 'I give you three months,' she said.

'Three months?' said Billy, startled.

'You'll be on your way soon enough. You're restless. And you've got more going for you than most.'

'Have I?'

'Of course.' She leaned towards him. 'You're bright, Billy,' she said. 'You've got it up here.' With this she tapped the side of her head, and then sat back again.

'I don't feel very bright,' he said. 'To be honest, I can't see a future for myself at all at the moment. I've dropped out, I have no qualifications, and I don't know anyone.'

'Nonsense. If you can't make your way on your wits and your charm, then there's something wrong with you.'

Billy smiled wryly. 'What charm?' he said.

'You're more attractive than you think.'

He looked down into his glass, and then at Beverley. The wine had lit up her face, and she was smiling in a way that was almost winsome. It dawned on him that her interest might not be so motherly after all.

'I suppose I am restless,' he said, attempting to get the conversation back on track. 'But I'm learning things. It's enough.'

'For now,' said Beverley, finishing his sentence for him.

The Tricksters' London debut was in the upstairs room of a pub near their flat in Earls Court. While the band members made their preparations, Sarah ordered pints of beer at the bar.

'I can't not drink with them,' she whispered to Billy. 'They expect it.'

He saw Julian coming down the stairs. 'How long have they been together?' he asked.

'Lee and Julian have been together for ages, but Andy and Art joined only a couple of months ago. They started out doing gigs at college.'

They made their way upstairs. The room was cluttered with amplifiers, speakers, wires and drums. The band took up their places, the guitarists tuning up, Art making a few precursory strokes, Julian tapping the microphone and counting into it. There were twenty or so people in the audience, of whom Billy recognized several from the party.

'Evening,' said Julian. 'Thanks for coming. We're going to play you a few... a few tunes. All our own work, as they say. The first song's called "Trick On You". A one, a two, a three, a four...'

The guitars and drums crashed in, and Julian cupped the mike in both hands. 'Trick on you,' he sang, 'I'm gonna play a trick on you, Gonna sneak up behind you, And play a trick on you.' Julian had a good voice, but he was forced to shout to make himself heard above the instruments. There was enthusiastic applause at the end of the song, and a cheer from Sarah. Billy placed his glass on the floor between his feet and clapped loudly.

The set came to an end, and they trooped back down to the bar.

'What do you think?' said Sarah.

'They're good,' said Billy, 'especially Lee. I like his voice when he comes in. He should do it more often.'

'Julian won't let him.'

'I'm not surprised.'

Lee joined them. 'You play like Clapton,' said Billy.

'Yeah? He's God, man.'

'No, he isn't,' said Julian, 'Jimi's God.'

'There are too many fucking gods around here if you ask me,' said Art. 'I'm going to find me some nymphs.' With this he turned and left the group, going to sit with a couple of girls who had been in the audience and were now eyeing them up.

During the second set Billy looked across at his sister now and then, at the smile of adoration that lingered on her lips. Why was it that Sarah had always gone straight for what she wanted, while he had taken the roundabout way? Was it as simple a matter as character? He thought of Peter's conviction that character didn't exist, or at least that it was formed by experience. And then he thought of Sarah at the age of two, of five, of ten: she had always been like this. He recalled how as a child she used to love eating overripe bananas. 'Lovely and bad,' she said of them, 'lovely and bad.' When, as he was leaving the pub, he turned back to see her kissing Lee, he felt a strange mixture of concern and jealousy.

———

Mrs Allingham was ghosting through the hallway one evening when Billy returned from work.

'How is your friend?' she said.

'I think he's OK. He keeps on having headaches, though.'

'What did the doctor say?'

'He hasn't seen one.'

She stood for a few moments as though lost in thought, and then beckoned him into her rooms. When they were seated she said, 'He must see a doctor.'

'I know. I've tried to get him to go, but he refuses.'

'He's wilful.'

'Yes.'

She stood and went into the kitchen, returning with a bottle of white wine. Without asking Billy whether he would like some, she poured two glasses and handed one to him. Billy tasted it, and it was very sweet.

'Some people find the problems of the world easier to bear than their own,' she said.

'I hadn't thought of it that way.'

'You don't, I take it.'

'My problem is not with the world, but finding my place in it.'

'Well, that's the problem of youth.'

She stared into the fireplace, and Billy took the opportunity to study her closely. He realized after all this time that she was beautiful, a desiccated beauty.

'I have this urge to know the world,' he said. 'All of it.'

'That would take a long time.'

'At least I know where I want to start.'

'And where is that?'

'Morocco. Marrakesh.'

'Why there?'

'I read a book about it, and it caught me.'

She sipped her wine delicately. 'The desert is very clean,' she said, 'like the jungle.'

'I want to see the shifting sands.'

'How is your French?'

'Passable.'

'You must know the language if you're going to be a traveller rather than a tourist.'

He placed his glass on the table. 'I'll brush up,' he said.

'When will you go?'

'When I can afford it.'

'I think you should be more definite than that.'

'Soon, then. I'll go soon.'

————————

'Sarah's been arrested,' Billy heard his father saying down the crackling line.

'What?' He turned to face the back of the hallway, cradling the phone closer to his ear. All his fears for his sister welled up inside him.

'Possession of Class B drugs. She's in Holloway Prison. What the hell's she been up to, Billy?'

'Can we see her?'

'Your mother and I are coming up tomorrow. Visiting time is eleven. You must be there too.'

'Of course.' Billy ran through his mind the excuses he might use with Wilson. 'I'll see you there.'

Holloway Prison was a crenellated affair reminiscent of the Tower of London. Billy shuddered as he entered the gates. His parents were already there, sitting on a bench in the waiting room. They stood when they saw him, and he kissed his mother and shook his father's hand. Their faces were lined with tension and fatigue. None of them said anything very much, and after a few minutes a warder led them into the visitors' room.

There were no iron grilles or glass panels, as Billy had somehow expected. Sarah sat at a long table, between two other women. The moment she saw them she burst into tears. Margaret held her in her arms, stroking her hair and whispering reassurances. Eventually they all sat down.

'It was horrible,' she said, wiping the tears from her cheeks. 'They just burst in, at midnight.'

'Were you taking anything at the time?' Jim asked.

Sarah shook her head. 'They found cannabis in the kitchen. They knew what they were looking for. If they hadn't found anything on us they'd have planted it.'

'So you've been smoking cannabis, have you?'

'Dad,' said Billy, trying to contain the anger he felt with his father, 'of course she's been smoking cannabis. Practically everyone smokes cannabis. It's harmless.'

'When I want your opinion I'll ask for it.' He turned again to Sarah. 'What's it like in here, sweetheart?' he asked.

Sarah groaned. 'I'm in a ward with nine other women. One of them's a child molester, or so they say.'

Jim let out a long, slow breath. 'A child molester?'

'We have to queue for everything – meals, baths, toilets. The warders come around four times a day and call out our names, just to make sure we're still there.' She looked around the high-ceilinged room. 'Where else would we be?'

'Are the warders all right?' asked Margaret.

'They're OK. Well, one of them's a witch.' She took a deep breath, and Billy could see she was taking courage from their presence. 'They strip-searched me when I arrived,' she said indignantly. 'Felt me up.'

'What about the others in the flat?' Jim asked.

'They're in Wormwood Scrubs, I think.'

'But what about your friend? Isn't she here?'

Sarah hesitated, and Billy said, 'She'd gone to her parents' for a few days, hadn't she?'

Sarah nodded. Jim stared at her intently, but remained silent.

'When do you come up for trial?' Margaret asked.

'I haven't been told yet.'

Billy banged his fist quietly on the table. 'They've no right to keep her here,' he said. 'It's a disgrace. Just because she's smoked some dope?'

His father gazed at Sarah, trying to muster more words. 'This is where they hanged Ruth Ellis,' he said eventually.

'Jim, for goodness' sake...' said Margaret.

'I'm sorry.' He looked down at his hands. 'It's just the

thought of my own daughter, in a place like this.'

'She's in a place like this because the system stinks,' said Billy, 'and for no other reason.'

'Let's not get excited,' said Margaret. 'Sarah, you'll be out of here in no time. Your father will talk to the police, and we'll have you home very soon.'

Sarah leaned across and hugged her mother. 'I'll be strong,' she said. 'I promise.'

Out in the street the wind swept them towards the car. As soon as they were under way Jim said, 'There is no girlfriend, is there? She's shacked up with a boy.'

Billy stared at the back of his father's head. There was nothing for it but to speak the truth.

'His name's Lee,' he said. 'He's very nice.'

'So nice that he gets himself and my daughter arrested.'

Billy sat silent now. He had said everything there was to say, and wasn't about to get into a pointless argument with his father. Margaret turned to face him.

'I'm sure you were keeping an eye on her,' she said.

'I was. But you know what she's like.'

His mother looked at him sorrowfully. 'Yes,' she said, 'I know what she's like.'

————

He sought the tranquillity of Hampstead Heath as often as he could. It was easy to lose himself in the woodlands and grassy spaces. But always he found his thoughts turning inwards. He was beginning to have doubts about Morocco. It seemed very remote, in every way. And what would he find if he did get there? Would everything somehow fall into place?

In time his walks became longer and further-reaching. And as well as his yearning to get away there was something else, something harder to define, which he could only describe as a wish to be understood. No one in his life really understood him, not his parents, not his sister, not Peter, not Mrs Allingham – no one. Surely there was someone who could tell him who he was and that it was all right? And as often as he recognized the impossibility of this, his longing for it always returned.

One Sunday morning, as he sat on a bench gazing at the first, improbably colourful rhododendrons near Kenwood House, his thoughts turned to Len Haskell. He knew better than to expect wisdom from Len; but he was family, he knew where Billy had come from. He walked back across the heath towards South End Green and the little house.

Len was unshaven and unkempt, and Billy sensed that he was the worse for a few drinks the previous night. He offered him a cup of coffee, and Billy stood staring out across the garden while he made it. Storm clouds were racing across the sky, and the first drops of rain speckled the windowpanes. Len returned to the sitting room and handed Billy a mug. He took a sip of the sharp, sour liquid.

'You made it just in time,' said Len.

Billy looked back out of the window. The rain was pelting

down now. 'We could do with some sunshine,' he said.

'We'll get it soon enough. You know what they say about the English weather, don't you – if you don't like it, just wait a few minutes.'

Billy tried his coffee again, but it tasted no better. 'Len,' he said, 'weren't you in North Africa during the war?'

'That's right. Why?'

'I want to go to Morocco.'

'Well, I never went there. We only got as far as Alexandria and Tobruk.'

'What was it like?'

'What was it like? It was a bloody nightmare. Hot as hell, sand in your eyes, Rommel's lot pounding away.'

'But wasn't it beautiful?'

'Not where I was, at any rate.' Len slurped his coffee and put down the mug. 'Maybe Morocco's different.'

'It's where the Sahara begins. The dunes.'

'It was flat in Libya. The only things that broke it up were the oases.'

'How long were you there?'

'About six months. Then they shipped us off to Sicily.'

'The sky must be big in the desert.'

'Big and blue. Always blue, day after day. Never a cloud in sight, as I recall.'

'I think I'd like that.'

'You would for a week or two.' He gestured towards the window. 'Then you'd start hoping for some of that stuff.'

Billy laced his fingers around the mug. 'Would I?' he said. 'I'm not so sure.'

———

Billy and Peter sat in the French House as though at a wake.

'It's not who pulled the trigger that matters,' said Peter. 'They're all in it up to their necks – the FBI, the CIA, LBJ.'

Billy couldn't help but find this succession of acronyms faintly comical, despite their occasion. The news of Martin Luther King's assassination had reached them only a couple of hours earlier. They had planned this night out several days ago, but now that they were here, Peter was morose and angry. Billy wanted to change the subject, but he knew his friend well enough now to sense that this would take some time.

'There'll be the usual inquest and the usual whitewash,' continued Peter. 'The killer was acting alone; he just felt like popping off a nigger; et cetera, et cetera.'

'Maybe not, this time,' said Billy half-heartedly.

Peter sniffed, as he always did when Billy said something he disagreed with but couldn't be bothered to contradict. They sat in silence for a while, Billy looking sidelong at Peter now and then. He had taken off his bandages, and there was little trace of his wound. But he'd had another dreadful headache only a few days ago, and Billy continued to worry about him. Peter shrugged off any enquiry about his condition with the assurance that he was fine, that a headache never did anyone any harm.

'Let's get drunk,' he said at last.

Billy looked at him in astonishment. He had never seen Peter have more than one drink at a time.

'Really?'

'Yes,' said Peter determinedly. 'I feel like getting drunk.'

'Getting drunk costs money,' said Billy, delving into his pockets to see how much he had.

'It's on me.'

With that Peter stepped up to the bar and ordered a bottle of wine. He splashed the glasses full, and raised his in a toast. 'To the revolution,' he said dully.

Billy studied Peter's face for signs of the irony he detected in his tone. It was always hard to tell anything from Peter's features: he had a very inexpressive face.

They sat drinking their way through the bottle, and then another. Billy was hungry by now, but something told him to let Peter dictate the course of the evening. He was also a little drunk, as Peter had intended, and when they stood to leave he was unsteady on his feet. They made their way outside, and wandered up Dean Street. Soho was in full swing by now, the coffee shops, restaurants and bars all doing a brisk trade. Outside the Phoenix strip club a bouncer said, 'Come on in, lads. Lovely girls.' Billy looked at the posters, at the girls in their sequins and not much else. He had never been to a strip club, and was sure that if they did so now they would be fleeced. Peter was on the same sort of wage as he was, and Billy had no intention of ruining him. After a while the only thing to do seemed to be to go to another pub.

They found one near Piccadilly Circus, and Peter ordered

another bottle of wine, ignoring Billy's protestations. When they turned away from the bar, Billy saw that two girls were looking in their direction. Before he knew it, Peter had marched across to them, placing the wine bottle on their table in a stagy way. Billy followed in his footsteps, and they sat down opposite the girls.

'Good evening, ladies,' said Peter grandly. 'My friend and I were admiring your…' He smiled vaguely, casting about him for words. 'We were admiring your coiffures.'

'Our what?' said one of the girls.

'Your hair, dear ladies.'

She ran her hand through her long blonde hair. 'All right, ain't it?'

'It truly is.'

Billy was appalled by this awful impression of David Niven on which his friend had embarked. He had never seen anything like it.

'Yours isn't so bad either,' said the other girl. 'Do you get it bleached?'

'This, my dear, is my natural colouring. Where I come from, the Barbary Coast, everyone looks like this.'

'The what coast?'

'Barbary.'

'Is that anything like the South Coast, then?'

The other girl, who was dark-haired and much prettier than the blonde, leaned towards her friend and said, 'No, it's like the Costa del Sol, that's what it is.'

'I am descended from slaves,' said Peter, settling into his assumed accent now.

'White slaves, that'd be,' said the blonde.

'The term "white slaves" strictly speaking refers only to females,' said Peter. 'For the delectation of the Moors.'

'What's the moors got to do with it?'

The dark girl nudged her friend. 'I think he's talking about the Moors murderers,' she said. 'Is he creepy, or what?'

'He isn't creepy,' said Billy. 'He's just a bit drunk.'

The girls directed their attention towards him now. 'So handsome's got a tongue too,' said the blonde.

'Look, let me buy you both a drink. My friend's had a bad day and he's letting go, that's all.'

'Perhaps he should let go somewhere else,' said the dark girl. 'Or maybe he shouldn't be allowed to let go anywhere.'

Billy stood up. 'Come on, Peter,' he said. 'We're leaving.'

'But what about the bottle of wine?'

Billy picked it up. 'We'll finish it at my place,' he said.

Peter got slowly to his feet. Billy grasped him by the arm, and they made for the door.

'Nice meeting you, boys,' said the blonde. 'Come and see us again some time.'

Out on the street they leaned against the wall of the pub, breathing in the night air deeply.

'You've got to work on your chat-up lines,' said Billy.

Peter hiccuped, and tried to bring him into focus. 'Have I?' he said. 'I thought that was a pretty good one.'

He met his father for lunch in a Chinese restaurant around the corner from the magistrate's court in Bow Street. It had been two weeks since Sarah's arrest, and only now was she coming up for trial. Billy had been fuming over all this, and when he'd gone back to Holloway to visit her a second time, he couldn't help but vent his anger at one of the warders. He'd been told to leave immediately, and had sat on the bus going home in a state of rage. But now, with his father, he was anxious to appear unconcerned.

'They'll let her off,' he said. 'It's her first offence, after all.'

'I hope you're right.'

They toyed with their chop suey, both too wound up to eat. After a while Jim said, 'I think I'm in trouble again myself.'

'How do you mean?'

Jim laid down his chopsticks and pulled a packet of cigarettes from his pocket.

'The Regal. It isn't paying.'

Sarah had alerted Billy to this, but he decided he had better act dumb.

'I thought it was doing fine,' he said.

'*Was*, yes.' Jim lit up, and directed the smoke away from Billy and the table. 'But not now. Television's just too strong a draw these days. And the costs of running a single cinema don't add up any more. At this rate I'm going to have to sell to Rank or somebody.'

Billy finished eating. He stared at Jim, uncertain how to handle this unexpected turn in the conversation.

'Are you sure about this?' he asked.

His father looked reflectively at his cigarette. 'I'm scared, Billy,' he said.

He had never seen his father like this. His image of him had always been one of a man who was sure of himself, irrespective of whether he was right or not. But Jim had messed up before. Billy had been too young then to understand what was going on. Now things were different, and he looked at a man who seemed vulnerable and uncertain. Billy was suddenly assailed by a sense of dread.

'If you have to sell out, will you get enough to repay the bank?' he asked.

Jim pursed his lips. 'Probably,' he said. 'But keeping up the mortgage payments on the house wouldn't be easy on the kind of wages I'd have if I were just managing it for somebody else.'

Billy recalled the day they had moved into their new house, the happiness they had all felt. At last he and Sarah and Tom had their own rooms, and weren't falling over one another all the time. Soon Sarah would leave home, and this would surely mean that Jim and Margaret and Tom could live in a smaller place. But Jim's pride was at stake again, and Billy knew what a force that was.

'What can you do to improve things?'

'I can let people go, so I don't have to pay them. It might

come down to me and the projectionist. Oh, and the ice-cream girl – she's on commission.'

'Should you be showing different kinds of films?'

Jim smiled wanly. 'That's what you always used to say when you spent your Saturdays there. You know Wells, Billy – the West End it isn't.' He called for the bill and stubbed out his cigarette. Looking up at Billy, he said, 'How are things with you, then? Still in London.'

'It looks as though I'll be here for a while. My piggy bank isn't very full.'

'Can't you apply for some kind of job in Marrakesh and then go out to it?'

'I have no idea what that would be. Anyway, I don't really want a job there, I want to have some time and freedom.'

Jim smiled again. 'Freedom, eh?' he said. 'I remember that. When you find it, hold on to it, that's my advice.'

He paid the bill, and they walked to the court. There was a long wait before they were led into the visitors' gallery. Sarah and the band sat on the front bench, facing three magistrates. The chief magistrate summoned the police officer who had made the arrests, and everyone sat through a leaden and self-justifying account of what had happened. The accused had drawn attention to themselves by their rowdy behaviour, he said. Billy found this very hard to believe, given the evidence of Sarah's birthday party, which even as he left it was subsiding into a mood of introspection and languor.

The defendants pleaded guilty, and the chief magistrate

pronounced his sentence. They were all put on conditional discharge. In view of her age, Sarah's condition was that she should return home to her family. Jim sighed audibly as the magistrate spoke the words.

They were reunited with her in the lobby, in a way that seemed to Billy rather confused. Sarah appeared from one door as they were coming through another. A policeman asked Jim who he was, and gave him a piece of paper to sign. It was all very perfunctory. Jim put his arms around her and held her tightly. She searched her father's face for signs of the censure she was surely expecting, and found none.

'Come on, sweetheart,' he said. 'I'm taking you home.'

Three

A few days after the trial, Lee appeared in the bookshop.

'I was around the corner in Denmark Street,' he said, 'looking at guitars. Then I saw the sign, and thought I'd drop by.'

Billy was glad to see him. 'Do you have time for a drink?' he asked.

He arranged with Beverley to take lunch early, and they walked to the Coach and Horses.

'What a lark!' said Lee as they sat down with their pints. 'Now we really are like the Stones – busted!'

'I don't think Sarah thought it was much of a lark.'

'I didn't have a chance to talk to her at all.'

'She had a terrible time in Holloway, banged up with a lot of crazies. What was it like for you?'

'We were in the Scrubs. It was a gas. We were all in the same cell. We practised close-harmony singing, until they shut us up.'

'Well, you had a better time than she did.'

Lee looked at him earnestly and said, 'Is she OK? I don't suppose I'll see her for a while.'

'I think you can assume she'll be under lock and key. Are

you going back to Wells any time soon?'

'No, we're going to Cornwall. We're going to get it together in the country.'

'Cornwall? Why there?'

'There's this old sawmill someone's turned into a recording studio. It sounds amazing. We're going to make our demo tape there.'

'Is the place really set up for that sort of thing?'

'Apparently. Julian's been there – it's not far from where his family live – and he says it's got the lot: four-track recording, a big control room. And it's much cheaper than the London studios.'

Billy had been wondering how they paid for things, especially since none of them appeared to have a job. 'How cheap is cheap?' he asked.

'Fifty pounds a week all in.'

'That doesn't sound very cheap to me.'

'Julian's paying for it.'

Billy gazed out of the window. The street was flooded with sunshine, and London seemed at last to have shaken off its winter blues. 'I've never been to Cornwall,' he said.

'Why don't you come, then?'

'Me? But I'm not a musician.'

'No, but you can help us out a bit. We can pretend you're the roadie. It'd be fun.'

'When are you going?'

'Two weeks' time.'

Billy thought for a moment. Would Wilson let him off for a few days? He'd been there only a couple of months. 'I'd love to,' he said. 'I'll see if I can get the time off.' He looked across at Lee, and a smile stole over his features. If he couldn't yet leave for Morocco, nonetheless he could still have an adventure.

———

Mrs Allingham invited all her boarders to what she termed a 'soirée'. Billy had generally kept out of the way of his fellow guests; but clearly he was going to have to talk to them now. With the exception of two middle-aged men whose occupations he could only guess at, everyone in the house appeared to be a student.

There were eight people in Mrs Allingham's bower, two or three having gone missing. She served the very sweet white wine she had given Billy, and handed around little skewers of diced beef and chicken. 'Dip them in the peanut sauce,' she said. 'They're delicious. Satay.' Billy wasn't sure whether 'satay' was what they were called, or some kind of salutation.

'Now, we have two literary types,' she said after a while. She turned to Billy. 'Have you met Simon?'

Billy shook hands with a fair-haired young man wearing baggy brown cords and a jersey with holes at the elbows. He had seen him on the landing, and had nodded cursorily, but they hadn't spoken.

'Simon is studying something very refined,' said Mrs Allingham. 'I don't recall what it is, though.'

'Medieval Italian literature,' said Simon, smiling. 'That means Dante and Petrarch, basically.'

'*Very* refined,' she said, waving her hand in the air and turning to talk to someone else.

'*The Divine Comedy*,' said Billy.

'*Very* divine, as Mrs Allingham would say. Not very comedic, however, at least not in the way we understand it.'

'Petrarch I know nothing about.'

'He was famous for his sonnets. He wrote them to someone he called Laura. Dante had his Beatrice and Petrarch his Laura. Except that Petrarch probably made up Laura.'

'Dante didn't make up Beatrice?'

'Not quite. He just made of her what he wanted.'

As they were speaking, one of the middle-aged boarders approached them.

'John Abbott,' he said, holding out his hand. 'Pleased to meet you.'

Billy and Simon shook his hand, and talk of Dante and Beatrice was shut down.

'At the university, are you?' he asked.

'He is,' said Billy. 'I work in a bookshop.'

'Do you now? I work in a shop myself, selling televisions.'

'That must be interesting,' said Billy idly.

'It certainly is. It's a booming market, I can tell you.'

'I don't watch it,' said Simon.

'Well, you should. I can fix you up with a nice Pye portable, cheap. There are educational programmes as well as the rubbish, you know.'

'I'm getting enough education as it is,' said Simon, smiling ruefully.

Billy felt a sudden urge to get away, and it dawned on him that it was Simon he wanted to get away from, not John. This encounter with someone who was studying something lofty had unsettled him. Very soon he made his excuses and returned to his room. He sat in his armchair reading, listening to the footsteps of his fellow boarders as one by one they made their escape from Mrs Allingham's rooms.

———————

Wilson sent Billy down to the basement for a few days. Philip was on holiday, and another assistant, Geoff, had what he described as pneumonia.

'*Pandemonia* more like,' said Peter. 'He should stay off the weed.'

The stock was completely new to Billy. By now he knew the fiction shelves from top to bottom, but here he relied on Peter to guide him. And then, after the second day, Billy realized that Peter seemed to be relying on him, asking him to do all the unpacking and shelving, and to mark the stock cards. Billy was by now accustomed to Peter's way of reading, which was to hold books within a couple of inches of his face. But now he sensed that something was different. And then there were the times when Peter would go to the lavatory and not return for twenty minutes or more. Billy began to watch his friend closely, sure that something was wrong, or at least more wrong than he had supposed. The next morning, when a box of Peregrine books was delivered, he decided to try something out. As he was unpacking he handed Peter a book opened to a particular page.

'I'm with Leavis on Spenser,' he said. 'Look what he says here about *The Faerie Queen*.'

Peter took the book from him and inspected the page. He smiled, and handed it back to Billy. 'Me too,' he said. 'He doesn't like Milton very much either.'

Billy tossed the book onto the counter. 'This isn't a Leavis,' he said. 'Look, Peter, come on, admit it: you can't read properly, can you?'

Peter looked at him blankly for a few moments, and sat down on the stool.

'It's double vision,' he said. 'I've been guessing for a week or more. It's a wonder nobody's noticed. You won't tell Wilson, will you? Please don't.'

'Oh, Peter!' said Billy. 'Do you mean to say that you're losing your sight and yet you still won't go and see a doctor?'

'I know. It's stupid. I'm sorry. I'm afraid, that's all.'

'Are you more afraid of doctors than you are of going blind?'

He looked up. 'I can't do it on my own,' he said.

Billy stared at his friend, his heightened sense of concern vying with exasperation over Peter's inability to take care of himself. He made Peter promise that they would together go to a doctor the very next day.

They went to the surgery near Peter's flat in Islington, and waited ages before he was permitted to register. The earliest appointment he could get was a week away. By then, Billy would be in Cornwall.

'You will be sure to go, won't you?'

'Yes, Billy. I promise.'

'Whose bright idea was it to go down on the Saturday of bank holiday weekend?' said Art, drumming his fingers on the steering wheel.

They were stuck in a traffic jam in the middle of Bodmin, and there was no end in sight to what had already been a frazzling journey. Billy was wedged between Art and Lee in the front of the Dormobile, and behind them the band's entire kit – amplifiers, drums, guitars, as well as rucksacks and suitcases – was stacked to the roof. Julian and Andy, the bass guitarist, had gone ahead the previous day in Julian's car, and to Billy the Dormobile felt like the band's packhorse.

Shortly before St Austell they turned south, and were soon descending a hill into the village of Golant. They came to a broad estuary, and parked the van facing onto it. There was a green MGB already there. 'Julian's,' said Lee. 'We're supposed to call him from here.'

While Lee went in search of the phone box, Billy walked

across a single-track railway line to the water's edge. Boats were moored everywhere, yachts and dinghies. Seagulls wheeled above him, cackling derisively. On the far side of the estuary the thickly wooded riverbank rose steeply into a bright blue sky. Billy stretched, glad to be free of the van and to taste the salt air. How far away was the sea? Not far, surely.

After a few minutes they heard the sound of an outboard, and saw a small boat approaching, towing a flat barge. Julian and Andy waved at them, and came alongside the quay and tied up. They loaded the contents of the van onto the barge and set off downriver, Billy marvelling at the strangeness of it all.

'You can't get there any other way except along the railway line,' shouted Julian above the din of the motor.

'Where does it go?'

'It's for transporting china clay down to the docks at Fowey. There's only one train a day.'

They soon turned towards the bank, and drifted under a bridge into a small creek. Ahead of them Billy saw a large, square building, with a verandah at the front. It nestled in the trees, flanked by tall pampas grass. Julian steered the boat to the jetty, and they arrived at the Sawmill.

It seemed the most improbable place for a recording studio. But as Billy discovered when they carried the amps and the instruments up the slope, it really was one. The control room was dominated by a console that sprouted buttons and lights. Beyond it was a room with bare stone walls and floor, in which microphones stood like stick-men in a child's drawing, and wires snaked all around. They set up the amps and drums, and placed the guitars against the walls.

The resident sound engineer was called Gord, and he made tea for them all. They sat on the verandah looking out over the creek. 'Isn't this a hoot?' said Lee, and Julian and Andy started making hooting noises, which then turned into a choo-choo riff. They were exhilarated, by the craziness of there even being such a place, let alone by their having it all to themselves.

Lee and Billy fixed supper, doing their best with sausages and mash. As darkness closed in, they set off down the railway line to the village and the pub. The Fisherman's Arms was a tiny nook, with a wrought-iron fireplace and an upright piano. The walls were hung with photos of Golant and Fowey in the past, of sturdy fishermen and their boats and nets. At the bar sat a man of about sixty wearing a smelly old coat. He scowled as the boys entered, and stroked his moustache.

'He was here last night,' said Julian. 'Calls himself the Major. Thinks he owns the place.'

They sat down at a table, and Andy and Art began to roll cigarettes, drawing out the ritual as though they were rolling joints. Julian went over to the piano and started singing 'Ballad of a Thin Man'. 'Because something is happening here,' he sang, 'But you don't know what it is, Do you, Mr Jones?' His fingers crashed down on the keys, and he ratcheted up the performance, making ironical faces as he did so. Then out of the corner of his eye Billy saw the Major step down from his stool and approach the piano. Without a word he grasped the lid in one hand and brought it down forcefully, Julian managing to withdraw his fingers just in time.

'This is for music,' said the Major furiously, and he swung on his heel and returned to his place. Julian clearly thought about raising the lid again, but came back to the table instead, muttering 'Fuck you' under his breath. The others sat staring at the Major, before Lee said, 'Anyone heard Dylan's latest?'

'*John Wesley Harding*?' said Julian. 'He's gone soft.'

'No, he hasn't. He's gone back to his roots.'

'You can't go back,' said Julian emphatically, swilling his beer in the mug.

'So why did he go electric in the first place?' said Andy.

'He went electric because the world's become a noisier place,' said Lee, 'and he didn't want to be drowned out.'

'Nah,' said Julian. 'He went electric because he started tripping on acid.'

They went on like this for an hour or so, scoring points off each other. When they stood to leave, Julian went up to the bar to buy a bottle of whisky to take back to the Sawmill. As Billy held the door for the others he saw Julian flick open his lighter and put it to a cigarette. Then, leaving the flame burning, he reached down and held it under the hem of the Major's coat. Facing the other way, and in his cups by now, the Major had no idea what was going on. A wisp of smoke curled up into the air.

'Night, all,' said Julian. He sauntered towards the door, and gave Billy a wink as he stepped outside. The last thing Billy saw as he closed the door behind him was the Major leaping from his stool and shouting, 'Fire!'

———————

The next morning the band set up in the studio, preparing to record their songs. Never having done this before, they relied on Gord to direct things. Billy sat with him in the control room, looking through the glass door to see them going about their work with expressions of anxious intent.

'They need to lighten up,' said Gord. 'Need to get used to being in a studio. We shouldn't try to record anything today.'

When they did come to record, there were frequent intermissions during which everyone crowded into the control room to hear what they had just played. The novelty of it was clearly intoxicating, and they grinned from ear to ear as they listened to themselves.

'There's a lot of bleed in this studio, I should tell you,' said Gord. 'The bottom end of Art's drums is bleeding into Andy's acoustic, and Andy's guitar delay is bleeding into Art's drum track. But that's no bad thing – it makes it sound real.'

Billy had no role to play, and after a while he began to feel bored and cooped up in the control room. He decided he would go for a walk, and set off down the railway line towards Fowey.

The china clay docks were vast, great sheds and hoppers lining the quay. The ships moored alongside seemed vast too, their names and ports of registration hinting at Poland and

Sweden and Italy. Billy walked through a landscape blanketed by a film of clay, quite at odds with the bright colours of spring on the far bank. And then he found himself in the town, strolling down a narrow, winding street. The houses were washed in pinks and blues and yellows. The wares of a ship's chandler spilled out into the road, and then there were clothes shops and fishmongers and cafés the size of broom cupboards. Whenever cars appeared, the pedestrians stood with their backs to the walls to let them gingerly pass.

He came out into the main square, and walked over to the railing to look across the harbour. The water dazzled in the sunlight, and Billy shaded his eyes so as to look out to sea. He turned around, to see that the town sloped steeply upwards, its roofs piled on top of one another. Directly in front of him was a pub, The King of Prussia, with a bow window like the prow of a ship. He went inside, bought a half of beer, and sat down in a corner.

There was something almost too pretty about Fowey, he thought. This was the Cornwall of the postcards, a place where fishermen mended their nets and hailed one another gruffly as they passed, where the publican wore tattoos all the way up his arms. But it was also a gateway to the world. The Italian ship would pass within a few miles of Morocco on its way home. Perhaps he could ask for a passage, or stow away? But, no, he must do things properly, and he must be patient. By the end of the summer, surely, he could make his plans and go.

The days passed, the band spending their time in the studio,

Billy taking walks in the woods or reading on the verandah. At low tide the creek was a stretch of sheeny mud, the water having receded even beyond the bridge, the boat and the barge lying stranded by the jetty. The rhythms of life in the Sawmill were in some ways fixed by the tides, and Billy liked this notion very much.

'It's my birthday today,' he said one morning over breakfast.

'How old?' asked Lee.

'Twenty. No more teens.'

'We must have a party, then.'

'Yeah,' said Julian. 'Let's get some booze in. How are we doing for dope?'

'We've got plenty,' said Art. 'I had a nice chat with my man in Notting Hill just before we left.'

They spent the morning in the studio, and then went into Fowey to plunder the off-licence. It was Julian who paid, as always, casually peeling five-pound notes from a wad in his back pocket.

'Thanks,' said Billy.

'It's not all for you, birthday boy.'

In the evening they sat at the table on the verandah, drinking and passing around joints.

'All we need now is a few chicks,' said Art.

'Some hope,' replied Julian.

Billy looked out across the water. 'I'm spending my birthday up a creek,' he said.

They talked on for a long while, until Billy decided he

needed some air. Lee followed him, and they sat on the bench. The moon was full, and its reflection lay in the black water just in front of them, seeming to be within touching distance.

'Do you know the story of the Moonrakers?' Billy asked.

'No.'

'They were some Wiltshire yokels raking a pond for kegs of smuggled brandy. When the excise men caught them they feigned idiocy and said they were trying to rake the moon out of the pond.'

Lee gazed up at the moon in the sky and then at the one in the creek. 'When I was in Kathmandu a kid asked me if we have the same moon in England as they have there.'

'You were in Kathmandu?'

'Sure, on the trail.'

'What was it like?'

'Pretty rough in lots of ways. But beautiful too.'

Billy looked thoughtfully at Lee. He had been to Kathmandu, had been somewhere utterly remote. Suddenly he saw him in a different way.

'What happened?' he asked.

'What happened?'

'I mean, how did you feel when you were there? Did it change you?'

Lee looked up at the moon again. 'That's hard to say,' he replied. 'I don't think you can know if you're changed, at least not until later.'

'I feel changed by places,' said Billy. 'I feel changed by this place.'

'In what way?'

'Oh, I don't know. It's so peaceful compared to London.'

'Is peacefulness what you're looking for, then?'

'Sometimes. And other times adventure. Both, really.'

They fell silent. Lee glanced back at the house, and then at Billy. 'I miss Sarah,' he said.

'She misses you.'

'I really mean it. I'm in love with your sister.'

Billy took some deep breaths, trying to sober up. 'Shouldn't you be trying to forget about her?' he said. 'She's still at school, after all, and you're miles away in London.'

'I can't forget about her. She's so lovely, so sweet-natured.'

Billy smiled. 'You should see her when she's in a temper,' he said.

'I can't believe she has a temper.' Lee turned towards the water again, his expression wistful and grave.

'I'm sorry,' said Billy. 'Nowadays you probably know her better than I do.'

'I've got to find a way to see her again.'

'There are other things you've got to do first, though. We should turn in – you need to be in good voice tomorrow in the studio.'

'I suppose so.' He put his arm around Billy's shoulders. 'Happy birthday,' he said.

———

His week was drawing to a close. Reckoning that it would take two days to hitch back to London – one as far as Wells, and the other the rest of the way – Billy planned to leave on Saturday. On the Friday morning they all took the boat into Fowey, tying up at the quay and setting off for the pub. There was a billiard table, and they competed with one another in their ineptitude. Billy felt at ease with them now, accepted, and he was sorry to be leaving. They returned to the Sawmill, Billy trailing his hand in the water.

As they ducked under the bridge he saw a girl strolling down the grass slope towards the jetty.

'Rachel!' said Julian. 'What the hell's she doing here?'

Lee turned to Billy and whispered, 'Julian's ex.'

He watched as the girl sat down on the bench. She had long dark hair, and was wearing a flowery dress with puffed sleeves.

'Hello, boys,' she said as they came alongside.

'What brings you here?' Julian asked.

She sat with her hands resting palms-down on the bench, rocking one leg on the other. Her boots were brown suede, and went up to her knees.

'I was visiting my parents, of course,' she replied. 'Your dad told mine you were here.'

They clambered out of the boat, and Julian gave the girl a chaste kiss. The others nodded in greeting, and Julian introduced her to Billy. She was pretty in a mournful kind of way, her lower lip drooping a little, her eyes shrouded with too much kohl.

'How long do you want to stick around?' asked Julian.

'Oh, I have to drive back to London today. You can make me lunch, and then I've got to go.'

They walked up to the house, and pottered around in the kitchen preparing salads and setting out bread and cheese. The atmosphere was strained, and it seemed clear to Billy that Rachel's presence was not entirely welcome. Billy found his eyes returning to her often, to this colourful figure who had landed in their midst. When they were washing up he said, 'I've got to get back to London too. I don't suppose I could ask you for a lift?'

She looked at him appraisingly. 'Well, if you don't suppose so, then I don't think I can,' she said. 'But if you *do* suppose so, then of course I can.'

———

Rachel's red 2CV was parked alongside the band's van. They unfastened the catches of the canvas roof and drove off in a cloud of smoke from the exhaust. Going up the hill out of the village the car stuttered now and then, and Billy wondered how it would get them all the way to London. But Rachel seemed a good driver, manipulating the strange gear-lever and swinging the steering wheel from side to side on the narrow lanes. Soon they were on the main road heading towards Truro.

'So how did you come to know the band?' Rachel asked.

'My sister's a friend of Lee's.'

'Y'know, they're not good enough,' she said, pulling out to

overtake a lorry. 'Oh, they can sing and play. But they need to write better songs.'

'They'll do it, won't they, if they take it seriously?'

'I'm not so sure. I've known Julian since school, and he's never taken anything seriously in his entire life.'

Billy braced himself as they took a bend a little too fast. 'And what do you do?' he asked.

'Do?' she replied. 'I don't *do* anything. I'm a poet.'

'Ah.'

'OK,' she said, softening. 'I *do* poetry. And you?'

'I work in a bookshop.'

'Great.'

'Not very. It's Collet's, on the Charing Cross Road. Do you know it?'

'I know where it is. I used to go into Better Books, until it became like everywhere else.'

'I've heard about the good old days of Better Books. They sound fun.'

'I went to a Stevie Smith reading there once.'

'I'm afraid I don't know her work.'

'She's my heroine. She writes poems that are down-to-earth.'

It was strange hearing her use a phrase such as 'down-to-earth', since that was the last thing she herself seemed to be. Presumably her family had money, like Julian's, which enabled her not to 'do' anything. He had been turning to face her now and then, and couldn't decide whether she was beautiful or not. There were moments when she seemed lovely, and moments when she seemed pouty and plain. He looked at her hands as they gripped the steering wheel. There were heavy silver rings on several of her fingers, and her nails were very long and bright red.

'What sort of stuff do you read?' she said.

'Oh, novels. I've been trying to discover new writers lately. I've been reading a wonderful book by Saul Bellow, *Seize the Day*. Heller, Nabokov, Baldwin.'

'They're all men.'

'Yes, I suppose they are. What about you? Besides Stevie Smith?'

She smiled sardonically. 'They're all women,' she said. 'American mostly – Sylvia Plath, Marianne Moore, Anne Sexton.'

'I need to read more poetry. I seem to be a prosy sort of person.'

'Do you know the difference between prose and poetry?'

'No, what?'

'Prose is words in the best order, and poetry is the best words in the best order.'

They stopped on the edge of Dartmoor for a cup of tea, and Billy took the opportunity to study her more closely. The kohl was definitely a mistake – she would look so much better without it. Her eyes were a deep green colour with flecks of brown, and he found himself looking at them closely.

'Where did you go to university?' Billy asked.

'I didn't. Went to a *lycée* in Avignon for a year. University's no place to be if you want to be a writer.'

'University's no place to be if you want to be a *reader*.'

'You too?'

'Oh, I went to Bristol for a year and a term. But I dropped out in February.'

'Good for you.'

This was the first time Billy had been congratulated on a decision the wisdom of which he was now beginning to doubt. 'I hope so,' he replied.

The journey was exhausting in the noisy little car, and the darkness put an end to their conversation. It was midnight by the time they reached London. Rachel pulled up at the bottom of Queensway.

'I live at the top of the street,' she said. 'Near the Porchester baths.'

'I can get the Tube home from here.' He grabbed his duffel bag from the back seat. 'Thanks for the lift,' he said. 'Perhaps you'd like to have a drink some time?'

'Sure,' she replied casually. She took a pen from her bag and wrote her phone number on the palm of his hand. Billy was struck by what he took to be the intimacy of this gesture. 'Give me a ring,' she said.

———

'You've missed all the fun,' said Peter at their coffee break on Monday morning.

'What fun?'

'In Paris. There's a revolution going on!'

Peter was at his most animated, his hair uncombed, his fingers continually pushing his glasses up the bridge of his nose.

'What's happening?'

'The students have occupied the universities, and they're closed down. There's fighting in the streets. But the thing is, the people are behind them – they're giving them food and blankets.'

Billy hadn't seen a newspaper in Cornwall or since he got back, and this news struck him as extraordinary. Perhaps Peter's prophecies were about to become real after all.

'There's this guy called Dany Cohn-Bendit who's leading them. He's got red hair!'

'He doesn't sound very French.'

'He's originally German. And a Jew.'

'It's true, Billy,' said Philip, sensing his scepticism. 'This time something's really changing. It's not just a student protest.'

'It's going to spread all across the country,' said Peter. 'And then to Germany. Just you wait and see.'

'And what about here?'

'Here?' Peter looked puzzled for a moment. 'Oh, we're not ready for it here.'

Billy went back to work, taking over from Beverley at the counter.

'They're all in a tizzy down there,' she said. 'No one's doing anything except nattering and arguing.'

'It sounds pretty exciting.'

'Is it?' She looked down the stairs to the basement. 'It's just boys being boys, that's all.'

It was a slow morning, as Mondays always were. Billy wanted to find out from Peter what the doctor had said, but would have to wait until lunchtime. He found his thoughts drifting towards Rachel. How many days should he let go by before he called her? It was ages since he'd last gone out with a girl, almost a year. Where would they meet? And how much would it cost to take her to dinner? He was lost in these thoughts when he became aware of a thump from the basement. There was a cry, and then Philip appeared at the top of the stairs.

'Peter's collapsed!' he said.

Billy raced down the steps, to find Peter sprawled on the floor. He had been carrying a pile of books, and they were strewn across the room. He was unconscious, and breathing only shallowly. Billy ran back up the stairs to find Andrew Wilson, but Philip had already got to him, and he was on the phone asking for an ambulance. They returned together to the basement, and crowded around Peter's inert body.

'Don't touch him,' said Wilson. 'Wait for the ambulance to arrive.'

It was ten excruciating minutes before it did, during which time Wilson closed the shop and the rest of the staff hung around not knowing what to do. Billy kneeled at Peter's side, looking for signs of movement or recovery, but seeing none. When the ambulance men arrived they stood back, and gently

Peter was laid out on the stretcher. Billy followed them up the stairs.

'I'm coming with you,' he said.

'Against the rules,' replied one of the men.

'Where are you taking him, then?'

'The Middlesex.'

Billy turned back into the shop and asked Wilson if he could take time to go to the hospital. 'Of course,' he said, visibly shaken. Billy set off up the street, following the sound of the siren.

At the hospital he waited for a long time before anyone was able to speak to him. Finally a doctor came to the desk, and the duty nurse nodded in Billy's direction.

'Are you a relative?' he asked.

'No. I'm a friend.'

'Do you know where to contact his family?'

Billy realized that Peter had never spoken of his family, nor indeed about his past at all. Why had he never asked?

'I'll ask the manager of the bookshop where we both work,' he said. 'What is it, Doctor? What can you tell me?'

'He's had a stroke brought on by a subarachnoid brain haemorrhage.'

'What's that?'

'It's a leaking of blood over the surface of the brain, under a layer called the arachnoid.'

A horrible vision of spiders flooded Billy's mind.

'We're going to do an angiogram. He will almost certainly

need surgery, and quickly. Has he suffered from high blood pressure?'

'Not as far as I know.'

'There are signs of a wound.'

'Yes. Could the stroke have been caused by a blow to the head?'

'Certainly.'

'Then that's what did it. He was in the Grosvenor Square demonstration, and a policeman hit him on the head with his truncheon.'

The doctor drew in a sharp breath. 'Why on earth didn't his GP refer him immediately?' he asked.

'Because he didn't have a GP,' replied Billy. 'I'm not sure whether he's seen a doctor since it happened. I tried…'

Billy felt suddenly overwhelmed with anxiety. He sat down on a chair.

'This is madness,' said the doctor. 'To have sustained a wound like that and not to have done anything about it?'

'I know.'

The doctor squared his shoulders and became businesslike again. 'I'd be grateful if you would try to let a relative know where he is.'

'Of course. I'll go to the bookshop now.' He stood and turned to leave, and then looked back again. 'When can I see him?' he asked.

'That depends on the success of the operation. Call the front desk when you have contact details for a relative, and the nurse will let you know.'

Billy walked slowly back to the bookshop, all sense of urgency having left him. It was open again, and he went straight to Wilson's office and gave him an account of what he had learned.

'Who can we get in touch with?' he asked.

Wilson threw down his pipe in a gesture of what seemed very like hopelessness.

'His parents are both dead,' he said. 'That's all I know. He's alone, Billy. He's completely alone.'

———

For several days, thoughts of Peter and Rachel contended in his mind. The only news from the hospital was that Peter had been operated on but remained in a coma. There was no point in visiting him until he regained consciousness. Billy wondered whether anyone besides him had attempted to do so. And when he called Rachel, she had seemed so offhand that he began to doubt whether he wanted to get together with her at all. He was scarcely in the mood for a date, given his feelings of guilt over Peter. He should have dragged him to a doctor much sooner: it was obvious that he had needed help. He went through his hours at the bookshop in a daze of worry and self-reproach.

The evening of his drink with Rachel came around, and they met in a pub on Westbourne Park Road, not far from where she lived. They sat awkwardly at a table near the door, Rachel continually looking up as people came and went.

'Have you heard any news from the Sawmill?' Billy asked.

'No. I don't expect to. Julian and I… well, I don't really know why I went there. We're not in touch these days. I suppose I was curious about this place he'd found.'

'You said you were at school with him. Where?'

Rachel slid a fingertip around the top of her wineglass, as if trying to set it humming. 'It was in St Ives,' she said. 'A private school called Penhaligon's, where everyone's father was a painter or a writer.'

'And which is yours?'

'A painter. He does naive seascapes.'

'And Julian's father?'

She smiled. 'A writer. Adrian Saunders. He writes stories of naval battles in the Napoleonic Wars. You must have them in the shop.'

'Of course. I hadn't made the connection. They sell pretty steadily. *Before the Mast*, and other titles I can't remember.'

'*Behind the Mast?*' she said. '*Up the Crow's Nest?*' She picked up her drink. 'I'm sorry, I'm being facetious.'

For a few moments he watched her in silence, and then he said, 'So what led you to poetry?'

'Oh, life.' She looked up at a stylish couple who were just coming through the door. When she failed to elaborate, Billy felt a wave of irritation pass over him.

'And poetry is what you do every day?'

She looked at him candidly. 'I was being provoking when I said that,' she said. 'I work part time in the gallery that sells my father's stuff.'

'Ah,' said Billy, feeling he had won a concession from her at last.

They went to a Greek restaurant, and ordered houmous and taramasalata and squid. This was a classier kind of place than Billy was used to, and he was relieved not to have to shout above the strains of bouzouki music and Zorba-like exclamations from the waiters.

'Now your story,' said Rachel.

Her directness was unnerving, and Billy found himself unsure how to reply.

'You have one, I presume?' she said.

'A sort of one.' He looked up at her. She was wearing too much kohl again, and it was smudged around her left eye, giving her a slightly piratical appearance. 'I'm quite ordinary compared to you.'

'I don't see how you can possibly say that. You barely know me.'

'OK. But your father's a painter and mine runs a provincial cinema. You're a poet and I work in a crummy bookshop.'

'It sounds to me as though you've got an inferiority complex.'

'Does it, now?'

She extended a hand to cover his. 'I'm sorry,' she said. 'I can be annoying, I know. Let's start again.'

Billy felt electrified by the touch of her hand. Suddenly he felt an urge to talk about himself, an urge he had suppressed for what seemed a long time now.

'My family is ordinary,' he said. 'I don't mean that bloodymindedly. It just is. My father bought a car dealership in Bath after the war, and for a few years it went very well. Then he over-extended himself, and went bankrupt. We moved to a farmhouse in the middle of nowhere in Somerset, and I went to a school the size of this restaurant. Later I went to a place called the Wells Blue School, and after my father took over the cinema we moved to Wells.'

'A country childhood.'

'I was much happier there than I had been in Bath. I was free.'

'We lived in the country, on a clifftop near St Ives. I used to walk for hours along the paths.'

'So you know what it's like, then, to be able to get away, to be yourself.'

'Yes, I do.'

Their moussaka arrived, and they fell silent for a few moments.

'Go on,' she said.

'So we lived in Wells. Do you know it?' She shook her head. 'It's a market town, but it has a beautiful cathedral. The school was pretty small even there. I read a lot, and did English at A-level. Then I went to Bristol.'

'And lasted a year.'

'A little more than a year.' He put down his fork and took a sip of wine. 'I'm wondering now whether I should have stayed.'

'Not if you still feel the way you did just a week or so ago.'

'I suppose so. I want to travel. But after that I don't know where I'm going.'

'Do any of us? I've no idea.'

'But you've got a vocation.'

She smiled wryly. 'We'll see about that,' she said. 'I've got a *calling*, shall we say.'

'Is there any difference?'

'One's a fancier word than the other.'

The conversation turned to writers, and to the ones they liked. As had been clear in the car, there was a great gulf between his reading and hers. Billy spoke again of Saul Bellow, whose novels he was now devouring. Then he sensed that he was boring her, and said, 'I must read some contemporary poetry. I stopped at Eliot and Auden.'

'There's a reading at the Indica bookshop next week. A friend of mine is one of the poets on the programme. Want to come?'

'Thank you.'

'I'm not sure what you'll think of it. She reads to the accompaniment of a saxophone.'

Billy gazed into her eyes, and all his doubts about this girl fell away. He wanted to see her again, and soon.

———

He went to the hospital for news, and was told that Peter was still unconscious.

'I'd like to see him anyway,' he said. 'Is that possible?'

The nurse led him down corridors and up stairs, and eventually they came to a room containing just two beds. One was empty, and in the other lay Peter. He had an oxygen mask clamped over his face, and was hooked up to fearsome-looking machines by wires that were attached to his head. His hair had been shaved off, and there was a gash along his skull where the surgeon had operated.

'I'll leave you alone for a few minutes,' said the nurse.

He sat down in a chair by the bed, and took Peter's hand in his. It seemed very warm, unnaturally so. In his terrible repose, Peter seemed far away, in another world. Was anything going on in that normally fervent mind? A graph on one of the machines showed a steady rising and falling of brainwaves or some such. Billy found himself stroking Peter's hand, and then raising his own to his face to brush away tears. He stood up, kissed Peter's forehead, and turned to leave the room. Then quickly he retraced his steps down the corridors and out into the street.

As he was climbing the stairs of the boarding house, he came upon Simon. On an impulse he said, 'Would you like to have a drink?'

'Absolutely.'

They went to the College Arms across the street.

'You look done in,' said Simon as they sat down.

Billy raised his fingertips to his temples, kneading them wearily. 'I've just been seeing a friend in hospital,' he said. He told Simon about Peter, about the demo and its aftermath,

realizing after a minute or two that he was talking compul-
sively.

'That's awful,' said Simon.

'Yes, it is.' He picked up his glass. 'But enough of this. Cheers.'

They drank their beer, and Billy looked at his companion. He
was very scruffy, his hair sticking out at odd angles; but there
was the light of a keen intelligence in his eyes.

'Tell me more about your studies,' he said. 'Our television
salesman put paid to that.'

Simon smiled. 'Do you really want to know?'

'Yes. Tell me about Dante and Beatrice.'

'It's a pretty well-known story.'

'Not to me, it isn't.'

'I'm sorry. I don't mean…'

'I know you don't.'

'OK. Well, you know that Dante was inspired to write *The
Divine Comedy* by his love for her?'

'Yes, more or less.'

'He first saw her when they were about nine. Then when
they were grown up, Dante fell in love. But he had no chance of
marrying her, or even meeting her properly. So he wrote
poems. He pretended they were to someone else, a screen-love.
Then he collected them in a book called *La Vita Nuova*, the new
life.'

'A screen-love?'

'Yes. It was a convention of the time. You concealed who it
was you really loved by writing apparently to someone else.'

'How odd.'

'Not really. The rules about courtship and marriage were very strict.'

'And *The Divine Comedy* came later.'

'Yes. After Beatrice had died young. But the earlier poems are more about the opposition between real and ideal love, about how lovers project on to their loved ones what it is they themselves desire, rather than what may be there.'

Billy's thoughts strayed to Rachel. What was it he was feeling for her? A sort of fascination, a sort of awe. Was this the way men were fated always to feel about women?

'If you want to know more about Dante and Beatrice,' said Simon, 'then come to a lecture. Outsiders are always welcome, and I've got a good tutor.'

The thought of stepping back into a lecture room made Billy shudder. 'Thanks,' he said. 'I'll think about it.'

———

The Indica bookshop was in Southampton Row. Its window displayed poetry and art books, and inside there were imports from America, from publishers such as New Directions and City Lights. Rachel introduced him to her friend, Dolly. She was dark like Rachel, but cultivated a more bohemian look. Her hair fell in ringlets around her face, and there were gold bangles on her wrists. The long black dress she wore set off her figure, and Billy found it difficult to keep his eyes away from her breasts.

She was one of three poets reading that night. The bookshop had laid on wine, which they drank from plastic cups, and people mingled and chatted for about half an hour before things got under way. They went from the bookshop itself into a room at the back, where the walls were lined with posters and paintings and the ceiling was covered with a strange silver material that shimmered whenever the door opened and closed. There were folding chairs set up in rows, and a single chair facing them at the front. A foppish-looking man with blond hair and horn-rimmed glasses stood and introduced the first poet. He was American, and he read his poems in a deep bass voice. Dolly was on next, and as she approached the front, so did a man holding a saxophone. Dolly coughed a couple of times and took a swig of wine, while the sax player tootled up and down the scales.

'I'm going to read a poem called "Cascade",' she said, and she rustled the pieces of paper in her hand.

'The music vibrated through my vagina,' she began, 'As though it were one of the instruments.' She paused, and the sax player sounded a few stricken notes. 'I felt myself becoming an orchestra, Becoming multicoloured. The sound ran through my hair like a celestial comb, It ran down my spine like a lover's caress.' The sax player did his thing again. 'I was a cascade of blue-green rainfall, I was a sonority of light.' She looked up, and the sax player remained silent. Someone in the front row began to clap.

Rachel leaned towards him. 'I think you'll find that owed rather a lot to Anaïs Nin,' she said.

Dolly carried on, the imagery of her poems becoming increasingly sexualized, her voice increasingly breathy. The sax player remained on hand, and contributed random notes now and then. Billy's thoughts drifted continually to Rachel, and now and then he stole glances at her. She seemed to be taking a supercilious kind of pleasure in the evening. He wondered what *her* poems were like, and whether he would get to hear them. It was one thing to criticize others' work, and quite another to stand up and read out your own.

They went to an Italian restaurant for something to eat, and Billy spent much of the meal worrying whether he was expected to pay for it. The dinner at the Greek place had cleaned him out. But it was Rachel who asked for the bill, saying, 'My turn.'

As they stepped outside into the street, Billy began to wonder when to say goodnight. Should he walk her to the Tube station? Should he buy her a nightcap in a pub? But she cut off his deliberations, turning to him and saying, 'Do you want to come back to my place?'

Her place was miles away, whereas his was just around the corner. She must know this, he thought. His pulses raced, and without thinking he said yes. She hailed a taxi, and very soon they were pulling up outside a block of flats in Bayswater.

The flat was enormous, and seemed all the more so for being bereft of furniture. Rachel led him into a sitting room that contained a single sofa, a coffee table and lots of books, mostly in piles on the floor. 'I don't know how long I'll be here,' she said, anticipating Billy's enquiry. Above the sofa was a poster advertising the famous poetry reading at the Albert Hall in 1965, when Ginsberg and others had read to thousands of people. Billy had heard about it, and wondered how poetry had sounded in a space so vast and so formal.

'Coffee?' said Rachel.

'Thank you.'

She went into the kitchen, and Billy followed her, leaning against the door pillar while she put on the kettle.

'Bloody cockroaches,' she said, taking off a shoe and slamming it down on the counter.

They returned to the sitting room, and sat on the sofa drinking their coffee.

'Were you at the Albert Hall?' he asked.

'God, no. I was still at school.'

She lay back against the cushions, and Billy sat immobile, cradling his mug in both hands. Rachel looked at him very directly, and suddenly he understood with absolute clarity that the moment had arrived. He put down his mug and leaned across to kiss her. She reached up and put a hand around his neck, pulling him towards her. Within a few moments they were all arms and legs, lips and tongues. There was nothing romantic about it, just a rush of blood and a powerful desire not so much for Rachel as to get it done, to rid himself of his shameful condition.

'I haven't got anything with me,' he said, breaking off.

'Do you imagine I'm not on the Pill?'

She stood up and took his hand, leading him into the bed-room. Like the sitting room it was almost bare, the bed and a clothes basket being the only things in it. The bed was rumpled, unmade since the previous night. She began to take off her clothes. Billy did the same, feeling that really they ought to be taking off each other's clothes. When she lay back he saw how boyish her figure was. Her dark pubic hair was a shock to him – the girls in *Parade* lacked such profusions. He lay beside her, and she rolled over and straddled him, imme-diately seizing his penis in her hand and sliding it inside her. She ran her hands through her hair, and Billy reached up to touch her nipples. 'Suck them,' she said, and she leaned forward towards him. They were very dark and very erect, and he felt like a baby at the teat. She rocked back and forth, and Billy felt himself getting close. He grasped her arms and rolled over, staying inside her as they fell. As he looked down on her, she smiled for the first time. 'Come, Billy,' she said. 'Come in me.'

When it was over they lay side by side, the fingers of one hand entwined.

'You don't have to ask,' she said. 'I seldom come myself.'

'Why?'

She shrugged. 'I don't know. Don't let go, I suppose.'

'You could take a little more time,' said Billy. 'And not jump on me.'

'OK, I won't jump on you next time.'

Billy stared up at the ceiling, and the thought that there would be a next time gave him as much pleasure as the thing they had just done. He smiled to himself, the smile of a loon.

Four

It was Wilson who told him that Peter was dead. A kind of fatalism had stolen over Billy in the previous week, as Peter remained in a coma, and all he felt now was an absence of feeling.

He asked for a few hours off, and walked back to his room. Recollections of Peter came in no particular order, the image of him lying unconscious in the hospital bed merging with that of him being drunk and lordly in Soho. It was Peter's passions he recalled most clearly, his denunciations of things he didn't believe in and his certainty about the things he did. However sceptical Billy might have been about Peter's ideas, he was bound to respect them. A few days earlier the news of Robert Kennedy's assassination had broken. Well, this was murder too, plain and simple. But what was to be done about it? If Billy had been with him in Grosvenor Square he might have been able to identify the policeman who had hit him. But he hadn't, and he knew that any attempt to seek justice would be futile.

Wilson had tracked down a cousin in Essex, and a funeral was hastily arranged. It took place on a warm Sunday afternoon in a crematorium in Kentish Town. The only mourners were the cousin, a woman of about forty, and the bookshop staff, and this made Billy feel even more desolate than ever.

There was the pretence of a Christian service, and Billy wondered what Peter would have made of it, Peter whose great hero had described religion as the opiate of the masses. The sentiments expressed by the priest and Wilson and the cousin were cloying, and Billy longed for it to be over. When at last it was, he took his leave quickly, walking towards Hampstead Heath and solitude.

He found himself in South End Green, and then heading towards Len Haskell's house. The net curtain was drawn back again, and a few moments later Len was at the door. He led Billy to the sitting room and went off to the kitchen to put on the kettle.

'Dreadful business,' he said when Billy told him Peter's story.

'Yes, dreadful.'

'I should have offered you something stronger.'

'No, that's all right.'

'I suppose it's no use me saying he shouldn't have been in Grosvenor Square in the first place?'

'No, it's no use saying that.' Why was he repeating Len's words like this? What was it *he* wanted to say? He looked at the photographs on the mantelpiece. 'What was it like when your wife died?' he asked.

'It was the end of things,' said Len with a kind of vehemence.

'I'm sorry. I think I'm being selfish. I don't want to bring back painful memories.'

'They never go away.'

He looked at his uncle thoughtfully. 'What really happened between you and Dad?' he said after a while.

Len took a digestive biscuit and crunched it between his teeth. 'Your dad?' he replied. 'We just didn't get along. We're different, that's all.'

'But you haven't seen him or even Mum for years.'

Len sighed. 'It wasn't about the bankruptcy,' he said. 'It was about Jim's philandering. But I don't know how much you know about that.'

Billy's thoughts went back to the day he had discovered his father with the waitress from Goody's. They had been in the car, parked in a back street in Wells, and Billy had crept up on them and seen them kissing. It was one of the worst moments of his life.

'I expect I know more than you think,' he said.

'I expect you do. Maggie should have stuck up for herself, should have told him it wasn't on.'

'I don't think that would have been very easy for her. My father is a hard person to confront.'

'Maybe not. Is he still fooling around these days?'

'I don't think so. He has other things on his mind at the moment.'

'What sort of things?'

Billy hesitated, and then said, 'He's got money problems again, so he says.'

A grim smile came to Len's lips. 'He can't hang on to it,' he said, 'that's his problem.'

'I don't think it's the same thing as with the garage, though. Seems to me he's a victim of changing times.'

'Well, we're all that.'

Billy placed his cup on the table. 'Why don't you go and visit them?' he said. 'Isn't it time to let bygones be bygones?'

'I'll think about it,' said Len. '*He'd* have to invite me, though, not Maggie.'

'I'll talk to him.'

'You talk to him. If he's willing to bury the hatchet, then so am I.' He looked at Billy, and then said, 'I'm sorry – unfortunate choice of words.'

Billy shrugged his shoulders. 'Peter isn't being buried,' he said. 'He's being scattered across Epping Forest.'

———

He had spoken to Rachel in the days after Peter's death, but had not seen her again. Memories of their night, of her dark hair falling across his face as he caressed her breasts, kept returning to him. But their physical coupling had not led to the sort of intimacy he had expected. She had remained out of reach, had resisted him even. So it was almost as a stranger that he greeted her outside Hampstead Tube station one evening, kissing her on the cheek and then thinking he should have kissed her lips.

It was truly summer now, the evenings long and lazy. They walked to the Poetry Society, and joined a crowd that was made up entirely of women.

'Men should read Stevie,' said Rachel. 'They would understand women better if they did.'

She had been referring to her as 'Stevie' all along, as a friend would. It seemed clear to Billy that there was an element of love in Rachel's feelings about her.

She couldn't have been more different from Dolly, a little woman in her sixties wearing a pinafore dress with a lacy white collar, her greying hair swept severely back from her forehead. She chatted for a long while before reading from her latest collection, a book called *The Frog Prince*. Her poems were simple and direct, and she sang them beautifully. Billy looked across at Rachel, who clasped her hands together on her lap and gazed at the poet dreamily. He had never seen such a softness in her.

There was one poem in particular that moved Billy, and from the first lines he felt himself to be possessed by it.

> Rise from your bed of languor
> Rise from your bed of dismay
> Your Friends will not come tomorrow
> As they did not come today
>
> You must rely on yourself, they said,
> You must rely on yourself,
> Oh but I find this pill so bitter said the poor man
> As he took it from the shelf

Crying, Oh sweet Death come to me
Come to me for company,
Sweet Death it is only you I can
Constrain for company.

After the reading Rachel queued to have the poet sign her copy of the book, lingering for a few moments in conversation until the woman behind her coughed politely. They stepped out into the warm night, and Billy suggested they walk to the heath. He took her hand in his, and they strolled towards Parliament Hill.

Sitting on a bench, Rachel rested her head on his shoulder. London glistened below them in the soft evening light.

'So when am I going to read some of your poems?' he said.

She rubbed her cheek against the cotton of his shirt. 'I don't know. Some time.'

'What are they like? What do you write about?'

'Oh, things. Feelings.'

He kissed the top of her head. 'You're being evasive again,' he said gently.

'I know.' She sat up, brushing her hair away from her face. 'The truth is, I haven't written very much. I… I'm not sure how good I am.'

'But you're starting out. And technique matters in poetry. Don't be hard on yourself.'

She curled herself into him again. 'I *am* hard on myself,' she said, 'as I ought to be. Sometimes I feel like a fraud.'

'Why a fraud?'

'Because I tell people I'm a poet when I've got a few half-decent poems in a notebook and that's it.'

'Then write more.'

'Oh, Billy, you don't know how hard it is. Have you ever tried to write?'

'Nothing more than essays.'

'Then you don't know. A poet has to look in the mirror every day.'

'Let me read those poems,' he said. 'Let's go home, and then some time soon let me read your poems.'

In the bed in her flat he whispered the little banalities of love. Was he in love with her? Or was it simply that the mask had slipped and she had come to seem vulnerable like himself? For the moment all that mattered was that they were falling asleep in each other's arms.

———

The bookshop was a forlorn place in the days and weeks after Peter's funeral. Billy recalled thinking that he had looked like a ghost the first time he had set eyes on him. Well, he was a ghost now, and seemed to be everywhere. Billy had been so bound up in his own ideas about Peter that he hadn't noticed the effect he had had on others. The basement was gloomy nowadays without the light of his ardour.

Billy's days were gloomy too. He was sad for himself, but sadder for the memory of Peter. As Wilson had said, he had been completely alone. He had surrendered himself to his cause, and in doing so had found meaning and a sort of companionship. But these were surely no substitute for friendship, and love. Peter's loneliness weighed heavily upon him.

When one day Lee bounded into the bookshop, Billy welcomed him like an emissary from the world outside. They went to 2i's for lunch, sitting at the table at the back that Billy and Peter had often claimed for themselves.

'How's it going?' Billy asked.

'Oh, OK.' Lee took up his knife and fork and began to tap them on the table, setting up a brief syncopation. Then he put them down again and said, 'We're not getting anywhere, though.'

'Why not?'

'Our demo tape keeps coming back from people. We've sent it to all the labels – EMI, Decca – and no one wants to talk to us.'

'The tape you made in the Sawmill?'

'Yeah. We thought it was great then. But when I listen to it now I'm not so sure.'

'Do you have any gigs coming up?'

'Just one, in a pub in Fulham.'

'So what are you up to?'

'Nothing much. And Julian reckons he can't afford to pay us any more. We'll have to get jobs again.'

'I'm sorry.'

'Oh, we'll figure it out.' He looked up at Billy, hesitated for a moment, and then said, 'How's Sarah?'

'Fine, as far as I know. It's hard for us to talk on the phone.'

'I tried calling, but your dad wouldn't let me speak to her.'

'That's not really surprising.'

'I know. But I miss her. You couldn't get a message to her, could you?'

'What sort of message?'

'That I'd like to see her. We're not at the place in Earls Court now, but I could give you a number.'

'Are you sure? Remember what I said when we were in Cornwall? And Dad was pretty definite about Sarah having no contact with you.'

'Please, Billy. I miss her.'

He looked at Lee for a few moments. 'OK,' he said. 'I'm going there for a weekend soon. Write your number down on a piece of paper and I'll give it to her.'

On his way back to the bookshop, Billy stopped by a newsagent. He glanced at a newspaper, and read a few paragraphs about Russian tank movements on the Czech border. He thought about buying it so as to read the rest of the story, but he had got out of the habit of buying papers, and put it back on the shelf. As he walked back to the shop, he felt the powerful presence of Peter beside him.

Rachel lay back on the bed, her hair splashed over the pillows, and he kissed her mouth.

'Would you want to go to Marrakesh with me?' he asked.

'I don't know you well enough to travel with you, Billy.'

He took a strand of her hair in his fingers. 'I suppose not,' he said.

'Why Marrakesh?'

'I've wanted to go there for ages. It sounds wonderful.'

'A friend of mine went to Tangier once. She said it was a dump.'

'Marrakesh is near the mountains and the desert. And then there's nothing for hundreds of miles.'

She took his fingers away from her hair and stroked them in hers. 'Sounds to me as though you've got the bug,' she said.

'Yes, I have.'

'Then you must go.'

'But how? I don't have any money.'

'Well if you're going to think like that, you'll never go anywhere.'

He fell back onto the bed, and swept a hand across his forehead. 'You really wouldn't come with me?' he said.

'Billy, I don't know what you think is going on here, but we're not together, not yet at least.'

He looked at their naked bodies. They had made love, and by now this seemed to him an apt expression for what it was they were doing.

'Not together?' he said.

'I mean we're not in a relationship.'

'No?'

'Don't be obtuse. We've slept together half a dozen times.'

'And that doesn't mean anything?'

'I didn't say that.'

'Well, I think we're together. I think I'm in love with you.'

She raised herself on one elbow. 'Oh, you silly boy,' she said. 'Stop talking about "love". Let's just have fun.'

A shiver of hurt went through him. 'Well, if that's the way you feel…' he said.

She leaned over and kissed him. 'You're too serious, Billy,' she said. 'Now, are you going to make the coffee or am I?'

He went home for the weekend, and he and Sarah dropped by Goody's café.

'He's getting worse,' said Sarah.

'How?'

'Oh, shouting at us over nothing at all. Going to the pub by himself and coming back drunk.'

'Drunk?' Nothing that Sarah had said so far surprised him; but Jim had never really been a drinker.

'Well, not falling-over drunk. But definitely the worse for wear.'

Billy looked around the café. Goody's had been taken over by teenagers in recent years, the shoppers going to the tearooms around the corner.

'Have you talked to Mum about him?'

'We talk all the time. She's beside herself with worry. But she never seems to say anything to him. When things get difficult she just retreats into Tom's world.'

She picked up a spoon, carving patterns in the sugar and then erasing them.

'I'd better talk to him, then,' said Billy.

'Oh, please do. We're all at the end of our tethers.'

Billy pulled a piece of paper from his pocket.

'I've got a message for you, from Lee.'

Sarah sat up straight, dropping the spoon into the sugar bowl. 'You *do*?' she said.

'He came into the shop the other day. He says he misses you, and tried to call, but Dad wouldn't let him talk to you.'

'He *did*? Dad never told me.'

'Well, of course he didn't.'

'Is this a letter?' she said, grabbing it from his hand.

'No, it's just his phone number.'

She turned in her seat. 'There's a phone box just over there. Can you lend me sixpence?'

Billy gave her the money, and immediately she was gone, dashing down the street. He sat drinking his coffee and wondering what he would say to his father. At supper the night before, he had sensed the tension in the air. This was his first return home since going to London, and he was having difficulty in picking up the signals his family were sending out.

It was only a minute or two before Sarah returned, looking crestfallen. 'He's not there,' she said. 'I'll have to go out later and try again.'

Billy studied her face for a few moments. She was seventeen now, but how often did he still see the seven-year-old Sarah in her, the little girl who had been so lost when they went to live in the farmhouse, and so lonely.

They finished their drinks, and Billy decided he might as well go to the Regal now, while Sarah returned to the house. Outside the cinema a poster was headed 'Coming Soon', and showed the helmet of an astronaut. '2001 : *A Space Odyssey*', it read. As Billy entered the foyer he saw Bert Dampler, the assistant manager.

'Hello,' said Billy. 'What are you doing behind the counter?'

'Amy left a couple of weeks ago,' he replied. 'I'm doing this every day now.'

Billy looked at his shiny bald head and girlish features. He hadn't changed a bit since Billy used to come here as a boy. Bert was a young-old man who seemed perfectly happy to live out his life within the narrow compass of the town.

'Dad in his office?' Billy asked.

'Yes. Just go on up.'

Billy knocked on the door, and his father called to him to come in. It was a tiny room, cluttered with canisters of film.

'Come to view the wreckage, have you?' said Jim.

'What wreckage?'

His father extended an arm and swept it around the room. 'The *Marie Celeste* of the cinema world,' he said.

Billy sat down in a chair.

'Is it that bad?'

'It's even worse now than it was when we came up to London. I've had to let go of Amy and Colin.'

'Who does that leave?'

'Me, Bert and Stan.'

'Can you manage?'

'Oh, I'll manage,' said Jim. 'I've done so before and I'll do so again.'

'But, Dad,' said Billy, a note of irritation entering his voice, 'you're not confronting reality. If the economics of how cinemas run are changing, surely you must do something about it?'

'Not confronting reality, eh? Funny, but I seem to have heard those words somewhere before.'

'Well perhaps there's a reason for that.'

'Oh, yes? And what would that be?'

His father's face was suffused with rage now, a rage Billy knew was directed not at him but at everything. How dreadfully familiar this expression was, how often he had cowered before it in the past.

'Have you talked to the Rank people?' he said quietly.

Jim raised his feet up onto the desk and took out a cigarette. 'Not yet,' he said. 'I'm going to see how the summer goes. There's some good films coming up.'

'2001,' said Billy.

'And *The Odd Couple*, with Jack Lemmon and Walter Matthau. Supposed to be hilarious. It had better be – we could do with a few laughs around here.'

Billy stood up and crossed to the window. The matinee westerns had ended, and people were leaving the cinema and walking up the road. They were kids, mostly, boys in posses of four or five. He turned back to his father.

'Why don't you at least talk to the Rank people?' he said. 'No harm can come of it. You could give the impression you're thinking of taking a new direction, or something.'

Jim tipped ash from his cigarette. 'The only new direction I'll be taking is towards the Labour Exchange,' he said.

Billy left his father to stew, and walked back to the house. Immediately he heard voices raised in the sitting room.

'You're not to see him again,' his mother was saying. 'Your father forbade it, and that's that.'

'But why?' said Sarah. 'Just because we got busted?'

'Because you're seventeen and he's twenty-one. Because you're still a child.'

'Is that what you think of me?'

'Oh, Sarah,' said Margaret. 'Just be patient. Why are you and your brother in such a hurry to grow up?'

Billy padded silently up to his room and closed the door behind him. It was going to be an age before Sunday afternoon came around and he could take the train back to London.

———————————

He knocked on the door of Rachel's flat, and to his astonishment found that it was Julian who opened it.

'Hi, Bill,' he said.

'Julian!'

He was wearing a lacy white shirt that was open practically

to his navel, and he looked very pale. There was a hint of make-up on his face.

'Come on in,' he said. 'I was just passing.'

They went through to the sitting room, and after a few moments Rachel appeared, holding two glasses of wine. She handed one to Julian, and turned to Billy.

'Wine?' she said.

'I thought we were going out.'

'We are. Later. Wine?'

'OK, thanks.'

She went back into the kitchen, and returned with another glass and a stool. Julian sprawled on the sofa, and Rachel motioned to Billy to sit next to him. She placed the stool on the other side of the coffee table, and sat with her long bare legs crossed, one foot hooked behind the other.

'How's tricks?' said Julian.

'All right,' Billy replied. 'Same as usual, really. What about you?'

Julian sat up and took a swig from the glass. 'We're breaking up,' he said. 'The band, I mean.'

'I'm sorry.'

He made a sour face. 'They weren't that great,' he said. 'I can do better on my own.'

'On your own?'

'Yeah. Singer-songwriter. Just me, my songs and an acoustic guitar.'

'What about Lee?'

'He's going back to the record shop in Bath where he worked before.'

'He must be disappointed.'

'I expect he is.'

Rachel had been sitting in silence, fiddling with her hair. When there was a pause in the conversation she said, 'Julian was picking up a book from me. Baudelaire.'

Julian grinned. 'Got to get my lyrics from somewhere,' he said.

'*Les Fleurs du mal*,' said Rachel. 'Weird.' She stood up and crossed the room, beginning to hunt through the piles of books against the wall. When she found the Baudelaire she placed it on the sofa beside Julian. He picked it up, leafed through it briefly, and then set it down again.

'So what are you two up to tonight?' he asked.

'We were just going to get something to eat,' said Billy. 'Maybe at the Greek place.'

'Disgusting stuff, Greek food. Don't know how you can stick it.'

Billy shrugged. 'We like it,' he said.

'We?' Julian turned to Rachel. 'I thought you hated it too.'

Rachel tossed her hair. 'Well I've changed my mind, haven't I?'

'A lady's prerogative.'

'Fuck off, Julian.'

He looked from Rachel to Billy, and then said, 'That's exactly what I was thinking of doing.' Raising himself from the sofa, he stepped around the coffee table. Rachel remained sitting on the stool, and he bent to kiss her, aiming for her lips. At the last moment she turned her cheek, and Julian's kiss landed on her ear.

''Bye, love,' he said, and to Billy, 'See you around.'

When he had gone, Rachel went to get the wine bottle and refilled their glasses. She sat next to Billy, leaning into him, and he put his arm around her shoulders.

'What was that all about?' he said.

'What was what all about?'

'Him. Julian.'

'I told you – he was collecting a book.'

Billy looked across the room, and then down at Rachel. All he could see of her was a tangle of hair. He took her hand in his.

'So how are you?' he said.

'I wrote a poem today.'

'You did? That's great.'

'We'll see.'

'Can I read it?'

'Not yet. It needs to ferment.'

'I'd like to, when it's fermented.'

'It might take a while.' She straightened herself, and then said, 'Shall we go to the Greek?'

'Are you sure you want to?'

'Oh, don't take any notice of Julian. Half of what he says is for effect, and the other half is lies.'

Simon gulped at his beer and placed the glass on the pub table, splashing some down the side. He was in a state of high excitement.

'I'm working on Petrarch's influence on Chaucer,' he said. 'It's extraordinary that no one seems to have done it before.'

'What's the evidence?' Billy asked.

'Chaucer refers to Petrarch in a poem, as the poet of the laurel crown. And he was in Florence shortly before Petrarch died. I'm sure they must have met.'

'The laurel crown?'

'Yes. Petrarch was the first poet laureate since the ancients. He went to Rome from Avignon to receive it.'

'Isn't Chaucer's stuff very different from Petrarch's?'

'That's what I'm working on. I think the influences are clearer than anyone has realized.'

Billy looked around the pub. It was a Monday evening, and the College Arms was empty save for themselves and a couple who were canoodling in an alcove.

'Did you say he lived in Avignon?' he asked.

'Yes. That's where he met, or imagined, Laura.'

'My girlfriend spent a year in Avignon.'

'I want to go there later in the summer.'

Billy's thoughts turned to Rachel, and to the strange evening they had spent a few days earlier. 'You were talking recently about the way lovers project the things they want on to their loved ones,' he said, 'whether those things are there or not.'

'Yes.'

'So that means that to be in love, you have to love two people.'

'Sort of.'

'Do you think they ever meet, those two people?'

'How do you mean?'

'Do you think that who she is and who you want her to be can coincide?'

Simon looked down into his glass. 'To be honest, I've no idea,' he said. 'I don't think I've ever been in love.'

'I can't tell whether I am or not. Sometimes I think so, and other times...'

'Don't we have to look at our parents to see what happens after a while?'

'Our parents? Are we really going to learn anything from them?'

'Well we ought to, surely.'

Billy cast his mind back to the weekend at home, to his father's rage and his mother's anxieties. 'Perhaps,' he said.

———

Rachel invited him to a party at Dolly's house near Ladbroke Grove. It turned out to be very grand, the biggest place he'd set foot in for a long while. He had somehow not expected Dolly to be rich. They went out into the garden, which was thronged with people, and were offered glasses of champagne by a black boy wearing a kaftan.

Dolly kissed Rachel, and held out a hand to Billy.

'So this is the young man,' she said, looking him up and down.

'The young man?' said Rachel.

'The young man you've been shagging. You have, haven't you?'

Billy felt his face colouring. Dolly might be unembarrassable, but he was not. Rachel twined an arm in his and said, 'And a very good shag he is too.' They both giggled, and Billy took a deep swallow of champagne.

They joined some people who were sitting on the lawn, and Billy half attended to their conversation, which veered from art to music to gossip. A paisley-shirted boy was holding court with four girls, talking about how he knew Donovan, how they were such good friends. They all seemed impossibly smart and sure of themselves. He lay back on the grass and watched the clouds scud across the sky, and then he closed his eyes. When eventually he sat up again, he realized that Rachel had disappeared. Dolly was sitting close by, watching him with a faintly amused expression.

'She saw Julian,' she said, 'and went off to talk to him.'

'Julian? He's here?'

'Apparently.'

He looked back towards the house, wondering what to do. The boy who had handed him the champagne came around offering hash brownies. Dolly took one for him and one for herself.

'So you and Rachel are having a good time?' she asked.

Billy bit into the brownie. 'Yes, we are,' he said. But as he spoke the words, he wondered whether they were really true.

'Has she shown you her poems?'

'Not yet. I keep asking to see them.'

Dolly arched her eyebrows. 'I wonder why?' she said. 'Perhaps because they don't exist?'

'Don't exist? What do you mean?'

She smiled, and made a show of inspecting her brownie closely.

'I have a feeling she hasn't written a single word.'

'How do you know?'

'I just know, that's all. It's obvious.'

'Not to me it isn't.'

'Well you're not a poet.'

Billy had an urge to say that she wasn't a poet either. There was something malicious in her expression now, and he knew he must get away from her. He stood up and walked across to the house, looking for Rachel. It was getting dark, and people were drifting back inside. Threading his way in and out of the rooms, he became aware that he was beginning to feel unwell. The hash brownie had been stronger than he'd realized. He sat down, and held his head in his hands. Suddenly he was overcome by nausea, and he stood and headed up the stairs. Feeling frightened as well as ill, he opened several doors in search of a bathroom.

Then he saw two figures emerging from a room at the far end of the corridor. Strange things were happening to his eyes, but he could tell that one of them was a boy in a lacy white shirt and the other a girl with long dark hair, hair she was in the process of brushing. He stood stock still, and then turned and ran back down the stairs. Stumbling out of the house, he was immediately dazzled by the streetlights. They seemed to be going around in circles, like a Catherine wheel. He climbed over a wall and lay down in a garden, but that only seemed to make things worse. After a while he decided the best thing to do was to sit up. One of the party guests, a middle-aged man, passed by him, and asked if he was all right.

'I just feel sick, that's all.'

'You had one of Dolly's hash brownies, I expect.'

'Yes.'

The man smiled. 'She makes the deadliest I know. The best thing you can do is get home and have some vitamin C.'

———

Sitting alone in the cinema in Leicester Square, half watching the images that flickered before him, Billy felt overcome by grief. He had lost a friend, and now he had lost a lover. Was life about something more than loss, and being lost? Two lovers kissed on the screen, and his thoughts returned once more to Rachel. She had been his first love, and would always be. But could he be sure that it had really been love, something more than just sex? When he had spoken of love she had said he was being silly. And then there was Julian. She wasn't over him, and hadn't been during the entire time she and Billy had been seeing each other.

When the film ended he stepped out into the warm evening and headed towards the river. The water was calm, untroubled by boats, and it lapped gently against the walls of the embankment. He looked across to the Festival Hall. A realization had been dawning for some time, and now he knew what he must do. His father needed him, and he had a duty to perform. Before he could think about going to Morocco, he must go home again. He walked slowly back to the boarding house and picked up the phone in the hallway.

Jim's voice sounded very distant on the other end of the line. 'What was that?' he asked.

'I said I'm coming home. I'd like to help you out in the cinema for a while, do some of the things Amy and Colin used to do.'

'You are? What's brought this on?'

'Nothing, Dad. I just think I can give you a hand.'

When he put down the phone he knocked on Mrs Allingham's door. She invited him in, and he sat down on one of the carved-wood chairs.

'I'll be leaving soon,' he said, 'once I've worked out my notice at the bookshop.'

'You're going to Morocco?'

'No, I'm going home. My father's got problems in the cinema, and I'm going to help out.'

'That seems very noble of you.'

'Does it? Perhaps. I thought I wanted to escape my family, but now I see that you can't do that, you shouldn't even try.'

'Blood is thicker, as they say.'

'Yes, it seems it is.'

Five

He lay in his bed, gazing around the room. The film posters had remained on the walls, Ursula Andress in *Dr No* and Julie Christie in *Darling*, and the shelves were filled with books by Orwell and Huxley and Hemingway. It was a teenager's room still. Sarah knocked on his door and said, 'Bathroom's free.'

'Do you always take this long?'

'I was only in there for five minutes.'

'Twenty, more like.'

'Well do you want to use it or not? Dad'll need it soon.'

He threw back the bedclothes and got up, grabbing his wash-bag. The bathroom looked as though three people had tried to use it at once, wet towels lying on the floor, shampoo and deodorant bottles standing open. Billy glanced through the steam at his reflection in the mirror, and his heart sank. What on earth had possessed him to come home again?

On the way to the cinema Jim said, 'So it didn't work out in London, then?'

'I didn't say that.'

They walked on in silence for a few minutes.

'What am I going to pay you?'

'I don't know. Pocket money. How about two pounds a week?'

'Are you sure?'

'The whole point of this is to *save* money, Dad.'

Jim looked ahead as the Regal came into view. 'All right,' he said. 'Two pounds a week it is.'

Bert Dampler was opening up as they arrived. They went through the foyer and into the auditorium, turning on lights as they did so. The floor was strewn with sweet wrappers, and the ashtrays in the arms of the seats were full of cigarette butts. Billy breathed in the stale air and said, 'I suppose this is where I start. I'll get the Hoover.'

He spent all morning cleaning the place, and then went home with his father for lunch. At half past one they returned to the cinema and prepared for the afternoon screening of 2001. Stan, the projectionist, had arrived, and was sorting out the reels of film. Stan was the longest-serving member of staff, having been there for years even before Jim took over. He was in his early sixties now, prematurely aged, and he shuffled around the place silently, exchanging only the most necessary words with the others.

Bert emptied a bag of change into the till and looked expectantly towards the door. Afternoon screenings on Mondays were never exactly crowded, but today there were just two people, a middle-aged man and a boy of about fifteen. Billy stood at the door of the auditorium and tore their tickets in half. When the film started, he dropped into a seat in the back row. The image of the spaceship preparing to dock at its station was stunning, the Strauss waltz crazy yet brilliantly apt. For an hour or more Billy sat spellbound, before it occurred to him that in fact he was working. He slipped back out into the foyer, to see his father talking to Bert. Jim turned towards Billy and said, 'I'm heading home for a while. I'll do the evening showing, and you can knock off once this one's over.'

'Is there anything I can do?'

'There's a consignment of chocolate bars that needs checking and putting on the shelves. Bert can show you.'

Billy spent a while at the sweet counter, and then went back into the auditorium. He had entirely lost the thread of the film, and simply surrendered himself to its images. The final scenes, in which the pilot flew through a kinetic corridor of light, were thrilling and terrifying. When it was over, Bert opened the doors, and the two paying customers stood and made their way out into the day.

'This one's so long we can only do two showings,' said Bert. 'Now I have to stick around until half past seven.'

'I'll stay with you.'

'Don't bother. There's nothing needs doing except minding the place. Stan'll go to the pub for his usual pint. Why don't you go with him?'

In all the years that his father had managed the cinema and Billy had helped out, he had never really talked to Stan. When he appeared from the projection room, Billy suggested he buy him a drink. The expression on Stan's face seemed to say that this could only mean trouble. They walked to the Rose & Crown, and sat down with their pints.

'So, how are you keeping these days?' said Billy.

'All right, I suppose.' Stan took a cigarette from behind his ear and rolled it back and forth between his fingers. Eventually he picked up a box of matches and lit it. 'I'm the one person your dad can't do without.'

'And he knows it.'

'Won't help me if he has to close the place down, though, will it?'

'He won't have to close it down.'

'Oh, no?'

'The worst that could happen is that he'd have to sell it.'

'Yes, to Rank. And the first thing they'll do is sack everyone and put in their own people.'

'You think so?'

'I've heard stories of the like.'

Billy watched as Stan smoked his cigarette. He did so very intently, as if he were trying to extract as much pleasure from it as he possibly could.

'Let's see what we can do over the summer,' said Billy. 'Maybe we can drum up some business somehow.'

'Best of luck,' said Stan. 'The place is doomed, and we all know it.'

————————

Sitting next to the director in the front row of seats in the Byre Theatre, Billy watched as his mother crossed the stage. Thomas More had just resigned as Lord Chancellor, and he and his wife were having a domestic moment.

'Luxury!' said his mother.

'Well, it's a luxury while it lasts…' replied More. 'There's not much sport in it for you, is there?… Alice, the money from the bishops. I wish – oh, heaven, how I wish I could take it! But I can't.'

'I didn't think you would.'

'Alice, there *are* reasons.'

'We couldn't come so deep into your confidence as to know these reasons why a man in poverty can't take four thousand pounds?'

The scene unfolded, More's daughter entering the fray. This was an early rehearsal of *A Man for all Seasons*, and the actors still read from their scripts. Afterwards Billy and Margaret walked to Cathedral Green and sat down on a bench. Wells was radiant in the evening light. He looked up at the west face of the cathedral and tried to tell himself that he was simply on his summer holidays.

'You were great, Mum,' he said.

'Oh, nonsense. I only got the part because I'm the right age. But I'm enjoying it nonetheless.'

He hadn't been alone with his mother like this since he returned. Sitting with her now in this lovely place gave him an unfamiliar sense of ease.

'How do you think Sarah is?' said Margaret.

Billy shrugged his shoulders. 'Fine, I think.'

'Not pining after that boy.'

'Oh, I'm certain she's doing that. But her exam results are more important than Lee, surely?'

'She thinks she did well.'

'She would.' Billy looked away towards the Dean's Gate. 'And Tom?' he said.

Margaret smiled. 'Tom is a treasure. It's his birthday next month. Don't forget.'

It was the middle of August, and he had been home for ten days. How long would he have to stay?

'You haven't talked much about London,' said his mother.

'I suppose not.'

'Did she hurt you, that girl?'

Billy looked down at his hands. 'Yes, I think she did.'

'You can't expect things to go smoothly at first. It's as much about discovering how to be with someone as anything else.'

'There are men my age who are married.'

'And do you suppose that's necessarily a good thing?' She turned towards him. 'Better to take these things slowly,' she said. 'You have lots of time.'

'Do I?'

'Of course you do.' She stood up, and smoothed down her skirt. 'They'll be expecting us back,' she said.

They walked across the grass, and Billy glanced at his mother. There was one member of the family of whom they hadn't spoken a word.

'Mum…' he began. 'Let's go to the Swan and have a drink.'

'If you like.'

They found chairs by the fireplace, and Billy set down two glasses of wine on the table.

'We haven't talked about Dad at all since I came home,' he said.

'No.'

'He's in trouble again, isn't he?'

His mother looked away from him. 'Yes,' she said.

'And this time it's harder, because he's older.'

'A lot of things get harder as you get older.'

'How is he with you?'

She looked up at him. 'I'm losing him again,' she said. 'He's drifting away, as he did after the bankruptcy. I don't know how to pull him back to me.'

'Can't you talk to him?'

She smiled wearily. 'You know what he's like,' she said. 'When he's in difficulty his main concern is to hide it, to pretend nothing's wrong. He shuts down.'

'But he's admitted to me that things aren't going well.'

'Perhaps it's easier for him to admit such things to you than to me.'

He looked at her intently. 'He's going to have to sell, Mum,' he said. 'The sooner he realizes it the better.'

'Oh, I think he knows that,' she replied. 'He'll do it in his own way and his own time.'

'No. He'll do it when his obligations to other people demand it. And if there's anyone who can tell him when that should be, it's me.'

She swirled the wine in her glass, and her face set suddenly firm.

'No, Billy,' she said. 'That's my task. He's my husband, and he must answer to me.'

'He's never done so before,' said Billy exasperatedly.

'Perhaps that's because I haven't been strong enough.'

'Don't be so hard on yourself, and so easy on him.'

She watched as the wine drained down the glass again, its rivulets glinting in the candlelight.

'I sometimes think I've spent an entire marriage being easy on him,' she said. 'And where has it got me?'

Billy had never heard such a note of bitterness in his mother's voice. He touched her hand. 'Things are going to have to change, Mum,' he said. 'And the first thing that's going to change is him.'

He backed the Vauxhall out of the garage, and Sarah hopped in.

'If Dad knew what I was doing he'd kill me,' she said.

'We're going to Bath to buy you the new John Mayall album,' replied Billy. 'You couldn't get it here, remember?'

'Right.'

They drove out of Wells in silence, Sarah gnawing at her fingernails and then fiddling with the radio. In the city, Billy parked in a new multi-storey car park, and they walked to the record shop. Lee's features broke into a broad smile as they stepped through the door. He and Sarah kissed and hugged each other, and they went outside.

'I'll see you in a couple of hours,' said Billy.

'Are you sure?' replied his sister.

'Of course. Where shall I meet you?'

'In the George,' said Lee.

They set off in their different directions, Billy heading towards The Circus. He had very mixed feelings about this city of his birth. Until he was ten years old he had lived in a large house near the London Road and gone to a private school with the sons of Bath's elite. Then had come his father's bankruptcy, and their move to the country. He had seldom returned since, and during the years of his growing up, Bath had become a tourist attraction. He sat down on a bench near the botanical gardens, wondering how Sarah and Lee were getting on. It was mad of him to have agreed to drive her here, but she had been pestering him ever since he came home.

He walked back into the centre, and sat in a café eating a sandwich and reading the paper. The Russians had finally invaded Czechoslovakia, and Dubček's brave experiment was over. Billy thought of Peter, and was somehow glad he wasn't alive to witness it. What was all this protest around the world amounting to, really? He set the newspaper aside. This reminder of Peter had sent a shaft of pain through him. If only he were here now, arguing and gesticulating. But moments ago, Billy had been telling himself he was glad he *wasn't* here.

He looked at his watch, and saw that it was time to collect

Sarah. Telling himself to snap out of this melancholy mood, he walked to the George. Lee and Sarah were sitting at a table in the furthest reaches of the pub, entwined in one another. Billy sat down, and they untangled themselves.

'What do you want to drink?' said Lee.

'Just a half of bitter, thanks.'

When Lee returned to the table, Billy said, 'Things all right in the shop?'

'They're fine. The manager said he'd take me back once, but not twice.'

'And what about your music?'

'I'm talking to another band. They're more bluesy. I'm hoping I can join them soon.'

As they were speaking, Billy became aware that someone had approached them. He looked up to see the lean figure of Bert Dampler.

'Hello,' said Bert.

'Hello. What are you doing here?'

'Taking my mother to lunch.' He gestured across the room to a woman who was waving at them. 'You remember my mother, don't you? She lives here.'

'Of course,' said Billy.

'What about you?'

'Sarah's buying an album. This is Lee, a friend who works in a record shop here.'

They nodded at one another, and Bert said to Sarah, 'Don't see much of you these days.'

'I don't seem to go to the pictures very often.'

'Nothing much on for teenagers. There's a shocker coming soon though, *Rosemary's Baby*.'

'Maybe I'll come along for that one.'

Bert returned to his mother, and the three of them went outside and said their farewells. Billy walked a few yards down the street and looked into a shop window. When Sarah caught up with him there were tears in her eyes.

'I won't see him again for ages,' she said. 'It's so unfair.'

They returned to the car, and Billy drove back towards Wells. Sarah continued to sniffle throughout the journey, staring silently out of the window.

'I told Lee when we were in Cornwall that he should try to get over you,' said Billy.

She turned on him. 'You did? Why?'

'Because it's hopeless, Sarah. You're here and he's there, and Dad's forbidden you to see each other.'

'He's not very far away now. I could take the bus.'

'But you'll need excuses. And Dad will suspect you're up to something.'

'It's all right for you,' she said, folding her arms. 'You're not in love.'

'Do you think I don't know how you feel?' he said, his voice suddenly tinged with anger. 'Do you think I don't miss Rachel?'

'Sorry.' She pulled out her handkerchief again. 'But you did say you weren't sure you were in love with her.'

'I *said* I wasn't sure. Now I think maybe I was.'

'Then you know how I feel about Lee.'

'Yes, I do. But that doesn't mean it's a good thing for us to see them again.'

'Why not?'

'Because there's no future in it,' he said earnestly. 'Because Lee is older than you and Rachel is mixed up.'

Sarah looked back at him. 'That's what boys always say about girls when they don't understand them,' she said.

Billy smiled. 'OK,' he said. 'Rachel is still in love with someone else.'

'Lee isn't, though. He's in love with me.'

Billy brought the car to a halt at a junction, and looked across at his sister, hunched in the passenger seat. 'Guess what I've just realized?' he said. 'You forgot to buy the record.'

———————

'Can't remember the last time I went to the pictures,' said Len. '*Lawrence of Arabia*, probably.'

'Is there a cinema near you?' asked Jim, refilling Len's wineglass and his own.

'There's an Odeon just up the road. But going by yourself's no fun.'

Margaret stood and began to clear away the plates. 'Coffee?' she said.

'No thanks, Maggie.'

Sarah and Tom had already got down from the table, and

Billy and Len and Jim sat toying with their glasses while Margaret went into the kitchen.

'Business not so good, then?' said Len.

'It's been better.'

'Got the place properly insured?'

'Of course I've got the place insured.' Jim picked up his glass, ignoring the stare Billy had been directing at him for several minutes now. He had clearly been fortifying himself since before Billy had collected Len from the station, and had been drinking steadily and purposefully throughout lunch.

'You can get insurance against the collapse of businesses these days,' said Len.

'Who said anything about collapse?'

Len shrugged, and knocked back more wine himself. His face was shiny with sweat, and he took a handkerchief from his pocket now and then to wipe his brow. 'I don't mean anything by it,' he said. 'Just trying to be helpful.'

'I've got all the help I need, thanks.'

'That's all right, then.'

Billy looked from one to the other, deciding that he'd had enough of this. 'Let me take you for a walk around the town,' he said to Len. 'You haven't seen it in a long time.'

'Is it any different?'

'Well, no. It's just a nice place to walk.'

At the last moment, Margaret said she would come with them. They walked to Market Place.

'That's where Dad once worked,' said Billy, pointing to a

shop whose sign read 'Underhill's: Outfitters to the Scholars & Gentry of Wells'.

They passed through Penniless Porch and into Cathedral Green.

'Hasn't changed, has he?' said Len.

'Now that's not fair,' replied Margaret. 'Not everything is Jim's fault. Life can be hard.'

They strolled across the grass towards the Deanery.

'I'm sorry I haven't been in touch,' said Len after a while.

Margaret placed her arm in her brother's. 'What matters is that you're here now,' she said.

'I'll come again, if you want me to.'

'Only if you want to. But you're going to have to try harder with Jim. You two rub each other up the wrong way.'

'Always have.'

'That doesn't mean to say you always have to.'

Billy turned to look at his mother and uncle. It had been difficult to persuade Jim to invite Len to Sunday lunch, and by now he was convinced it had been a mistake.

'This is the most beautiful façade of any in England,' he said, gazing up at the west face of the cathedral.

'It could do with a good clean,' said Len.

They returned to the house, and Billy drove Len to the station. When he got back he found his father slumped in his armchair, a half-empty bottle of red wine beside him.

'That was a great success, then,' said Billy.

'Is that my fault? I invited him into my home, and all he could do was gloat over my problems.'

'He didn't gloat, Dad. As he said, he was trying to be helpful.'

'Funny way of being helpful.'

'Oh, for God's sake!' said Billy. 'When are you going to face up to your responsibilities?'

'I am facing up to them. I'm running a business.'

'Yes, running it into the ground.'

Jim took a swig of wine. 'If you don't like the way I'm doing things you can clear off again,' he said.

'You seem to be forgetting that I'm trying to be helpful.'

His father looked at him with a strange expression that mingled resentment and fear.

'And you seem to be forgetting that I'm your father,' he said.

———

As the summer drifted on, Billy found himself mostly doing the evening shift in the cinema. During the days he reread his Conrads and Lawrences, and took long walks out towards Glastonbury and Shepton Mallet. At home, Jim's brooding discontent hung over everything, a discontent that occasionally found its expression in furious rows over very little. An uneasy peace existed between father and son, one that neither appeared to have any wish to breach.

Strangely it was Sarah who got on Billy's nerves the most. There were the typhoons in the bathroom, the constant refrain of 'Piece of my Heart' from her bedroom, the entreaties repeated every few days to find another reason for a trip to Bath.

Within a month or so of coming home, he was bored stiff.

There was no sign of an upturn in his father's fortunes, and he began to wonder how much longer he ought to stick around. Part of the problem was that he had no friends in Wells any more. And then one day he bumped into Roger Sealy in the High Street. Sealy had been the scallywag of his year at the Blue School, a little kid with curly red hair and a nose for trouble. Billy hadn't seen him since before he'd gone to Bristol, and they arranged to meet one evening for a drink.

'Did you know the school is moving?' said Roger when they sat down. 'The old building's being given to the Operatic Society.'

'No, I didn't.'

'Sad, eh?'

'I suppose so. Can't say I ever had a great love of the place.'

'Nor did I, but you know – nostalgia and all that. We had some good times there.'

'Yes, we did.'

'Remember when the Beak caught us smoking in Lovers Walk?'

Billy smiled. He had smoked twenty cigarettes in an hour as a dare, and had been ill for days afterwards. But it had cured him of smoking for ever.

'And when we broke into the school at night,' continued Roger, 'and hung girls' panties and nylons from the chandeliers in the assembly room?'

'My sister still wonders where those panties went.'

'We had fun, that's what we had.'

'So what are you doing now?'

'Apprentice printer at Pettigrew's.'

'How is it?'

Roger pulled a face. 'It's a job, isn't it? I'm getting married soon.'

'Congratulations. Who to?'

'Pauline Trudgian. Remember her?'

Billy shook his head.

'I was going out with her when we were in the sixth form. You must remember her. She had pigtails and glasses then, but she was always gorgeous underneath.'

'Yes, I remember now. You claimed to have slept with her the night before her sixteenth birthday.'

'Well I did.'

Billy gazed across the room. This conversation was heading exactly where he knew it would, nowhere at all.

'So what about you?' said Roger. 'We all thought you were going to be a professor or something.'

Billy picked up his glass and took a long draught of beer.

'I dropped out of Bristol and went to work in a bookshop in London,' he said finally. 'Then my dad needed some help in the Regal, so I've come home for a while.'

'And after this?'

'I don't know. I want to travel.'

Roger looked at him with a perplexed expression. 'And where's it leading?' he said.

'Where's it leading? That's a very good question.'

'What's the answer, then?'

Billy looked up at him. 'I wish I knew,' he said. He gazed across the pub at the other drinkers. 'Don't you wonder some-times what it's all about?'

'What what's all about?'

'Life, I mean.'

'It's about getting set up and getting on, isn't it?'

'But once you've set yourself up. Once you're established as a printer and you and Pauline have got kids…'

'That'll do me.'

Billy knocked back the rest of his beer. What was the point in musing aloud like this? Roger Sealy was one of the lucky ones, for whom it was all quite simple. Why did life seem to Billy so complicated?

———

Billy and Tom sat watching Dr Who, Tom making great play of hiding behind the sofa whenever the Daleks appeared. In half an hour Billy would need to set off to the cinema for the evening showing. Margaret had left for the theatre, and his father hadn't yet returned for supper. When eventually he appeared in the hallway it was clear that he'd been drinking.

'Sarah!' he roared. 'I want a word with you. Now.'

He came into the sitting room, looked hazily at Billy, and said, 'You too.'

Billy switched off the television and told Tom to go to his room. He knew very well what this must be about. His father went into the kitchen, and reappeared holding a whisky bottle and a glass.

'Looks to me as though you've had enough,' said Billy.

'Does it, young man? Well I'll be the judge of that.'

Sarah appeared and sat down on the sofa, folding her arms.

'You lied to me, both of you,' said Jim. 'I told you never to see that boy again, and what do you do but have a little tryst behind my back.'

'You've got no right to say I can't see him,' said Sarah.

'While you're living in my house I've got every right to. But the thing I don't like about this is that my son and my daughter lied to me.'

'Don't be so bloody sanctimonious, Dad,' said Billy. 'They had lunch together. If it had been anything more, I wouldn't have taken her.'

Jim looked at him with bleary eyes. 'But she'd have gone, wouldn't she?' he said. 'She'd have jumped back into his bed at the first chance.'

'You're disgusting,' said Sarah. 'I'm not listening to any more of this.'

She stood up and marched out of the room, banging the door hard behind her. Jim placed the glass and bottle on the coffee table and sat down heavily.

'I don't want my daughter to be a tramp, that's all,' he said.

Billy's own anger had been kindling, and suddenly it caught light. 'Do you know what you are?' he said. 'You're a hypocrite.'

Jim looked up at him in surprise, and took a slug of whisky. 'Just listen to the preacher,' he said.

'I'm serious. Do you think Mum didn't know about all the girlfriends when we were kids, the receptionists in the show-room, the waitress at Goody's?'

His father rested his elbows on his knees and looked vaguely across the room. The expression on his face was turning from anger to confusion.

'So I made some mistakes,' he said.

'You certainly did. One after another.'

'But Sarah's seventeen, and she's a girl.'

'Listen to yourself, Dad. What were your little sweethearts, if not girls?'

'There hasn't been anyone for years.'

'And that makes everything all right? That means Mum can just forget all the hurt, just pretend nothing happened?' He was furious now, all the repressed anger he felt towards his father spilling out. 'You're so bloody selfish you can't see anyone else, can you? You haven't got a clue about what other people might be feeling.'

Billy got up and stepped across to the table, picking up the bottle and glass and placing them on the sideboard. He sat down again and stared at his father in silence. Tears were start-ing in Jim's eyes.

'You don't know what it's like yet, Billy,' he said. 'You get married, you think you're in heaven for a while. Then a kid comes along, and suddenly you're second in the queue. She's too tired, she's got aches in all the wrong places. A girl makes eyes at you, and you're helpless.'

'You're not helpless,' said Billy. 'That's the point.' He sat rigidly in his chair, refusing to be softened by his father's distress.

'Have you never felt helpless?'

'Not over a girl, no.'

'Well just wait till you are. Then you can lecture me.'

'I'm not lecturing you about what you did ten years ago, I'm lecturing you about hypocrisy now.'

Jim took out a handkerchief and wiped the tears from his cheeks. 'It's easy for you to talk about hypocrisy,' he said. 'You haven't lived, haven't had to make compromises.'

'I know it when I see it.'

'Talk to me about hypocrisy in twenty years' time.'

'I will. But in the meantime I think you owe Sarah an apology.'

His father looked up at him, clearer-eyed now. 'Maybe I do,' he said. 'But don't you think a father has a right to be concerned about his daughter sometimes?'

Billy stared at his father, his anger subsiding now. 'Concern is one thing,' he replied. 'Constraint is another.'

———

The man from the Rank Organisation, Malcolm Dent, was very sleek, in a beige summer suit and a striped tie. Jim walked him around the Regal, Bert and Billy following at a respectful distance. Then they closed up and went to the Swan for lunch. At the corner table they sat studying menus and sipping water. Billy felt profoundly uncomfortable, but his father had insisted he join them.

'Baron Rank would like Wells,' said Dent. 'Old-fashioned values, that's what he believes in.'

'Perhaps Wells is just too old-fashioned,' said Jim. 'Perhaps we need some new ideas here.'

'Baron Rank is a traditionalist in his values, but has always been forward-thinking as a businessman.'

'So how did he create his empire, then?'

'By degrees. When he started, the scene was dominated by American films and distributors. But what he's most proud of is Pinewood, and the films that are made there.'

'*Brief Encounter*,' said Billy.

'Yes, *Great Expectations*, and many others.'

'And now you've taken over the Carry On films,' said Bert.

'Family-friendly films,' said Dent. 'Always family-friendly. And now perhaps you'd like to join the Rank family yourself?'

'Perhaps,' said Jim. 'This is just an exploratory conversation, you understand.'

'Naturally.'

Their first course arrived. Billy could sense his father willing Dent to order something other than water to drink, but no such word came from his lips.

'Economies of scale,' he said. 'That's what you're missing. You're paying through the nose for the films you're showing. If you were part of the Rank Organisation you'd save hugely on your costs.'

'But we'd just be a cog in a wheel,' said Jim.

'A vital cog in a very big wheel.'

After lunch, Bert and Billy returned to the cinema to open it up for the afternoon showing of *The Odd Couple*.

'What do you think?' said Billy.

'I think he's got no choice.'

'And what will that mean for you and Stan?'

'He's made a promise he would insist on us keeping our jobs. Whether he can deliver on it's another matter.'

'It wouldn't make sense to do anything else, would it? And Stan's close to retirement.'

'We'll see.'

Stan had arrived, and was fussing over the reels. There was a good audience for a weekday afternoon, about fifteen people. When his father came back, Billy followed him up the stairs to the office.

'So?' he said.

'So what?'

'Is he interested?'

'Of course he's interested. Now we have to do a little fandango for a while, that's all. They're not getting this place for nothing.'

———

'This is where I used to go to school,' said Billy.

He and Tom were sitting on the stone wall of a footbridge, below which flowed the bright water of a stream.

'It's a house, not a school,' said Tom.

'It used to be a school.'

Billy gazed at the little building, clad in the scarlet Virginia creeper he remembered from his first weeks there. What had then been the playground was now occupied by a small boat on a trailer. The sea was miles away, and he wondered when it was ever afloat.

'What did you learn there?' Tom asked.

'Oh, lots of things. About King Arthur and his knights for one.'

'King Arthur?'

'Yes. He's buried in the abbey at Glastonbury, or so they say.'

'I haven't been to Glastonbury for ages. Can we go now? Can we climb the tor?'

Billy smiled at his brother. He hadn't intended this to be a sentimental journey, but now that it was turning out that way he didn't mind at all. He had been two years older than Tom was now when they had come to the village of Coombe, and from the moment he had first set eyes on the tor he had known he was in a magical place. Would Tom sense that magic too? He couldn't remember the last time they had taken him to Glastonbury: he must have been very small.

They walked back to the car, and Billy drove down the narrow lane that led to the Glastonbury road. Memories of the harvest season ten years ago, of his early explorations, came back to him with extraordinary clarity. He had been a townie, and had had to learn the ways of the country. Now he was a townie again, and the landscape seemed to him once more charged with mystery and possibility.

They parked near the tor, and began the long climb up its western slope. There was a hazy light today, and it wasn't possible to make out many of the landmarks. They sat down on the grass and looked northwards towards Wells.

'Where is King Arthur?' said Tom.

Billy gestured behind them. 'In the grounds of the abbey,' he replied. 'We'll go there later.'

'So did you come here a lot?'

'No. Remember, I told you, Dad wouldn't let me. And we didn't have a car.'

'Didn't have a car?'

'Not everyone has a car, you know.'

'But we do.'

'Yes.'

Billy lay down and closed his eyes, thinking back to the windy spring day when he and his father had first come to the tor. The distance from Coombe had seemed too great to cross until then, but now it was utterly abolished, by the car, by the passage of time. It was hard to recall how much he had yearned to come here, and how long his father had refused his yearning. Was his wanting to go to the dunes nothing more than an act of revenge?

He sat up. 'I'll have to be leaving again soon,' he said.

'To ride the camels.'

'No, back to London, at least at first.'

'When will you go?'

Billy shaded his eyes, looking for the farmhouse where they once lived. 'I don't know,' he said. 'I have to help Dad for a bit longer.'

'After you've gone, I'll help him.'

'You'll have to wait until you're a little older. Then you can do what I used to, working on Saturdays.'

'I'd like that. I'd get to see all the films.'

'Not the grown-up ones, you wouldn't.'

'I'd sneak in.'

Billy smiled at his little brother. 'I expect you would,' he said.

———

Jim parked near Marble Arch, and they walked to the offices of the Rank Organisation. Malcolm Dent led them across the lobby and into a lift. His office was small and neat, and it was immediately clear that he was not in fact very senior.

'Mr Voysey will call us when he's ready,' he said.

They waited for fifteen minutes, Dent making small talk for a while and then falling silent, moving pieces of paper around on his desk. Eventually he led them into a much larger office, and a brisk man in a dark suit stepped around his desk and shook their hands.

'Do sit down,' he said. 'I trust Malcolm has been looking after you?'

'Yes, thank you.'

Billy looked across at his father, and sensed his discomfort. In the car he had been talking of how hard a bargain he had struck with them. But now he was clearly intimidated by the grandeur of his surroundings and the easy elegance of his new employers. Billy fiddled with his collar, wishing he could take off his tie. He hadn't worn one in years, and it was like having a noose around his neck.

Voysey crossed his legs and inspected a highly polished shoe.

'Welcome,' he said. 'Welcome in more ways than one. We have the papers here for you to sign. And once you've done so, you will be a member of the Rank family.'

Jim smiled weakly. 'I look forward to that,' he said.

'Good, good. And then we'll have your cinema brushed up in no time at all. They'll be flocking to it.'

'I'm sure they will.'

'Malcolm will be supervising the refurbishment. And reviewing your staff arrangements, of course.'

'We've discussed all that.'

'Yes, I know. And naturally we want to do our best by your people. We can't guarantee anything, however.'

'I've entered into this determined that I'll keep my team.'

'Quite right too.' Voysey stood and crossed to the desk, returning with a sheaf of papers. He placed them on the coffee table in front of Jim. 'Would you like a pen?' he said.

Jim produced a fountain pen from his pocket and inspected

the contracts. After a minute or so he signed both copies. Voysey took one and left the other on the table.

'Congratulations!' he said. 'This deserves a drink. Malcolm?'

They raised their glasses of sweet sherry in a toast to the future of the Regal. After ten more minutes of pleasantries they were back out on the street, Jim clutching the pieces of paper that foretold his future.

'Right, drink,' he said. 'And not bloody sherry.'

They found a pub on the Edgware Road, and Jim ordered large whiskies.

'Thank God that's over,' he said as he sat down.

'That part of it's over, anyway.'

'Come on, Billy, knock it off.'

'Sorry.'

'You know what? I'm relieved. Now someone else can worry about balancing the books.'

'They'll balance. These people know all about that sort of thing. But what about your books? Are you going to be OK?'

Jim knocked back his whisky and set down the glass on the table. 'The purchase price pays off the bank, with a bit to spare,' he said. 'And we can manage on what they're going to pay me.'

'Good.'

'This isn't like last time. I've learned a thing or two since then.'

Billy looked thoughtfully at his father. Perhaps he *had* learned things since the bankruptcy after all. It was so easy to think of him as being feckless; maybe by now this was unfair. Jim took a chequebook from his pocket and wrote in it, handing a cheque to Billy. It was made out to him, and for a hundred pounds.

'What's this?'

'Arrears.'

'What do you mean?'

'I mean you've worked in the cinema for two months for beer money, and this is what I owe you.'

Billy had never seen such a sum. 'Thank you,' he said.

'Now go and spend it. Go to Morocco, if that's what you want.'

———

Margaret strode across the stage and embraced her husband. In this scene, which formed the emotional climax of the play, she was by turns tender, indignant and hurt. Thomas More would soon be ascending the scaffold, the most illustrious victim so far of Henry's whims. And before the rigged trial commenced, he was saying his farewells to his family. Billy watched from his place in the front row. By now he had become very involved, helping his mother with her lines at home and turning up towards the end of rehearsals. Tonight they walked from the theatre to the Swan, and sat with their coffees and brandies looking out towards the cathedral.

'She was a brave woman, Alice More,' said Billy.

'She was devoted to her husband, and she never wavered in that.'

'She's not the only woman devoted to her husband.'

Margaret looked down into the brandy glass, her face

flushing. After a few moments of silence Billy said, 'What was Dad like when you first met him?'

She smiled. 'Cocky. He never had any doubt I would marry him.'

'And did you have any doubt?'

'No, of course not. There was a kind of madness in the air. The war was over, and if you were young you got hitched as soon as you could. It was only two months from when Jim and I first met that we were walking up the aisle.'

'And then the madness passed.'

'Yes.' She looked up at him. 'I know you think I've been indulgent,' she said, 'that I've let Jim get away with too much. But he's not a bad man, Billy.'

'What does that mean, not a bad man? How many people are bad, really? He's just weak.'

She took a sip of brandy. 'I did think of leaving him once,' she said, 'if I'm honest.'

'When was that?'

'The first time he strayed. I was carrying you.'

Billy thought back to the confrontation with his father, to the words about finding himself second in the queue. 'It wouldn't have been very easy, to leave then,' he said.

She looked up at him, her face darkening. 'It would have been impossible,' she said. 'It would have been ruinous.' She sighed, and composed herself once again. 'But enough of all this. Are you ready for Saturday?'

He looked at her steadily, wondering whether to press her

further, and realizing that he mustn't. 'I've got my passport and my train ticket as far as Madrid,' he said. 'Then I'll improvise.'

'How long do you think you'll be gone?'

'Until my money runs out.'

'And then?'

'I'm not thinking about "then", Mum. I'm going to have an adventure at last.'

Six

Billy woke to the muezzin's plaintive call to prayer, drifting across the rooftops from the mosque. He opened the shutters of the tiny window onto the faint light of a Moroccan dawn. He had arrived at Marrakesh station in the dark, after an exhausting three-day journey, and this was his first sight of the city. He could see very little, though – a patch of sky, a wall, and a single cypress tree. He turned back into the room, surveying the mattress on the floor and the leather-covered chest that were its only furniture. He dressed hurriedly, stepped out onto the balcony, and looked down into the court-yard. In the daylight he could see how dilapidated the house was, tiles broken or missing, the fountain clogged with dirty water. The young man who had greeted him last night, Adil, called to him to go up to the terrace on the roof, where he would bring breakfast.

Billy found the staircase, and went up to the top of the house. From the terrace he could see all across the city. The minarets were the only tall buildings, the rest being an apparently continuous structure faced with baked red mud. Adil brought him bread and honey and sweet mint tea, and he sat down on a rickety chair to eat it. Once the voices from the mosques had subsided, all he could hear was the disputatious chatter of tiny birds.

'You are tired,' said Adil. His French was fluent, and Billy knew he would have to work hard to keep up with him.

'Yes. It's been a long journey.'

'You must rest today, not try to do too much. I have to walk to my home soon, through the souks, and will take you if you like. Then you must spend the rest of the day here.'

He was a young man, in his early twenties, Billy guessed, his manner courteous and grave. He wore a striped and hooded gown that went down to his sandals. His complexion was pale, his forehead high, his face long and thin.

The driver of the horse-drawn carriage Billy had taken from the station had brought him here, through a maze of dark alleyways, assuring him that he knew a place that was clean and cheap. Billy had made himself a promise not to resist blandishments or invitations of any kind. He would be a traveller, and would give himself up to whatever experiences might present themselves. But as it turned out he had made a good start. The Dar el Magdaz was indeed very cheap, and Adil very welcoming.

Billy walked over to the other side of the terrace, and behind an awning he saw a startling sight, a great wall of snow-covered mountains that rose up, as it seemed, out of the southern edge of the city. His very first glimpse of mountains had been of the Pyrenees, from the train to Madrid. But this was an altogether grander sight. It made Glastonbury Tor seem like a bump.

'The Atlas,' said Adil.

'But they're so close.'

'They seem closer than they are.'

'And beyond them, the Sahara, no?' How extraordinary, that he should now be so close to his ultimate goal.

A couple of hours later, Adil led Billy out into the alley and towards the souks. The narrow streets were teeming with people, all of them moving quickly, looking intent on their destinations. A donkey-cart appeared, and they had to stand back for a few moments to let it pass. It was piled high with sheepskins, which gave off a tremendous stench. A blind man stood at a corner, his hand held crookedly out, utterly immobile and silent. Now and then Billy lost track of Adil in the crowd, and had to hurry to catch up with him.

They entered a covered passageway, and Adil turned to him. 'This is where the souks begin,' he said. 'You must never worry about getting lost in here. It is important to get lost. Eventually you will see a familiar place, and be able to find your way out.'

They strolled along the main street of the souk, surrounded at first by textiles, then by carpets, then by jewellery. The aroma of spices filled the air. Billy felt almost overwhelmed by this riotous assault on his senses.

Above their heads was an iron trellis that almost entirely shaded them from the sun. There was one kiosk after another, all jammed into the tight space, all offering the same things. How did they ever sell enough to make a living, wondered Billy, given how many of them there were? The faces of the merchants seemed to come in two kinds, the pale ones, like Adil's, and the darker ones, the faces of the mountains and the desert. Then there was the occasional Negroid face, a reminder of Africa. They looked at Billy without curiosity, and none made any attempt to accost him, perhaps because he was with Adil, perhaps because he was clearly too young and too poor.

Something jarred Billy's back, and he turned to see four men carrying a stretcher at shoulder height. For a moment he wondered what it was, before realizing from the outline beneath the colourful rug that it was a body. The bier continued on its way, its bearers shoving people aside as they went.

They passed stalls selling slippers and leather goods, and came out into the sunlight.

'When you return,' said Adil, 'look up now and then, and go always south. Now, I will show you the loveliest place in Marrakesh.'

They crossed an open space, weaving past piles of rubble and rubbish, and came to the entrance of a building that, from the outside, was as plain as any Billy had seen. Walking down a long corridor, they came out into a courtyard. Along two sides ran columned arcades, and in the middle was a shallow pool. Every inch of the surface of the walls was decorated with carved wood, stucco or tiles, and it was exquisitely beautiful.

'This is the *medersa*,' said Adil, 'the Koranic school. There are *medersas* everywhere in Morocco, of course, but I believe this is the most beautiful.'

'This is where boys came to learn the Koran?'

'Yes. As many as eight hundred, all living in tiny cells on the upper floors.'

'Eight hundred?'

'Yes. They were only boys, after all.'

'And they studied the Koran all the time?'

'All the time, and only the Koran. No other books were permitted. There are still many places in the country where you will find boys receiving a Koranic education. We are a very traditional society even now.'

'What about you?'

'Me?' Adil smiled. 'I am studying engineering at the university.'

'Ah.' Billy felt suddenly very humble. From the moment he had met Adil the previous night he had known that he was intelligent and thoughtful. But now he understood that Adil's work at the hostel was rather like his own in the cinema.

They sat on chairs under an arcade, absorbing the atmosphere of the place. Tourists came and went, their cameras devouring the scene, and Billy gazed above their heads at the delicate tracery of the carvings. Someone had said that the French described Morocco as the 'nearest of the far lands'. For the first twenty years of his life, Billy had not left his own shores. Now he found himself in a place as exotic as any he could possibly imagine. The sun rose above the rooftop, drenching him with its warmth. He closed his eyes, scarcely able to contain his excitement.

He sat in the Café de France, writing in his notebook and occasionally taking a sip of cold coffee. He had found his place, somewhere he could sit for hours on end, watching the world go by. The main square, the Djemaa el Fna, stretched away into the distance, crisscrossed by people on foot, in carts, on bicycles, and the occasional moped. Here and there were snake charmers and magicians, but Billy knew that the real show in the Djemaa got started only in the evening. Now and then, beggars with sad, haunted faces would step up to him from the street, holding out their bowls, only to be shooed away by the waiters. The children were more persistent, extending their hands in supplication, saying 'eat, eat' repeatedly, their sadness turning to laughter in a moment.

The men sitting at the other tables took little notice of him, speaking to one another in low, guttural tones. They greeted one another in a highly ritualized way, kissing four times on the cheek, bowing slightly, their right hand placed on their stomach. Billy revelled in his invisibility, scribbling in his notebook and then gazing out across the square, his mind empty save for the impressions of the moment.

A young couple arrived, looking around and then settling on the next table. Billy knew they were American before they uttered a word. The girl was very blonde, with a square face and cool blue eyes, and the boy very dark. Billy had read

about the hippy trail in Morocco, but these two were altogether too eager and fresh-faced to be dope-heads.
They ordered tea and sat studying a guidebook, writing
postcards, and counting their money. Billy did his best to
ignore them, but after a while the girl turned to him and
said, 'Sorry to disturb you, but my pen's run out. Can I
borrow yours?'

Billy handed her the pen, and a few minutes later she gave it
back.

'What are you writing?' she asked, her eyes resting on the
notebook.

'Oh, nothing. A journal. Of sorts.'

'There's a lot here to write about.'

'Yes, there is.'

'Are you staying long?'

She was very direct in her manner, a kind of earnestness
imbuing her every word and gesture. Billy could sense that he
wasn't going to be able to shake her for a while.

'I've only just arrived,' he said. 'I'm not sure how long I'm
going to stay.'

'My name's Erin,' said the girl. 'And this is Brad.'

'Hi,' said the boy. 'Glad to meet you.'

'Would you like to join us?'

Billy smiled. 'I'll lose my table,' he said. 'Let's just move them
closer together.'

'You're British?' said Brad.

'Yes. And you're American.'

'I guess we stand out.'

'No, I didn't say that.' He paused for a moment. 'Have you been here long?'

'In Marrakesh, just a couple of days. But we've been travelling in Morocco for more than a week. Started in Casablanca, and then went on to Fez.'

'What's Fez like?'

'It seems kind of... I don't know, kind of older. There's more going on here.'

'And where are you going next?'

'Oh, back to Casablanca, before we go to Senegal.'

'What will you be doing there?'

'We've joined the Peace Corps,' said Erin, a hint of pride in her voice. 'We're going to help with rural development.'

'What does that involve?'

Before she replied, they picked up their things and moved the two feet to Billy's table.

'The main crop is groundnuts,' said Brad. 'But they don't know how to export them. We're going to be part of a programme that'll help them to do that.'

'Sounds exciting,' said Billy.

'It is.'

Erin reached out to the notebook and opened it at the first page.

'Erin!' said Brad. 'That's private.'

She smiled. 'The storks in their lavish nests,' she read. 'That's good. You're a writer.'

Billy gently extracted the book from her hands. 'No, I'm not,' he said. 'I'm a traveller.'

As he was placing the notebook on the ground beside him, the air was suddenly rent by the call of a muezzin, summoning the faithful to afternoon prayer. They watched as the men in the café paid their bills and walked across to the mosque. It quickly filled up, and many of them had to lay out prayer-mats in the square. They faced east, bowing repeatedly, their foreheads touching the ground, their hands wrung together.

'It's a shame we can't go into the mosques,' said Brad.

'It's a shame *women* can't go into the mosques, even their own,' replied Erin.

'Things are different here.'

'They sure are.' She turned to Billy. 'We've been thinking of eating at one of the food stalls in the square, but we haven't taken the plunge yet.'

'Nor have I.'

'We could go together one evening, maybe.'

'Sure,' said Billy. 'Let's do that. I'm invited to someone's house tonight, but perhaps tomorrow.'

'You're invited to someone's house?' said Erin. 'Neat! How did you manage that?'

'There's a student who's the sort of caretaker at the place I'm staying. His family live in the old city, and they've asked me to supper.'

'Great. Tell us about it tomorrow night. Shall we meet here around seven?'

'First we must go to the *hammam*, the baths,' said Adil. 'Western-ers are not usually allowed into them, but you are with me.'

They were walking through the souks, past pyramids of spices and piles of figs and dates and oranges. It was early evening, and the narrow streets were crowded with people. Everyone seemed more interested in one another than in buy-ing anything from the stalls. Billy found himself thinking back to Market Place in Wells, and more recently to Portobello Road. But these memories seemed to be in black and white, so pale were they in comparison to the colour and intensity of Marrakesh.

Beyond the souks they walked along alleyways in which children played hopscotch and kicked small bundles of twine. Eventually they came to a recessed doorway and entered into a dark space. Adil exchanged a few words with the porter, and Billy saw a note change hands. The porter looked at Billy and gestured to him to enter.

As his eyes became used to the light, he saw that he was in a sort of ante-room, in which men's gowns hung from hooks and slippers were placed neatly under a bench.

'Take off everything but your underpants,' said Adil, 'and then take two of those buckets and a bar of soap.'

They stepped through a wooden door into another room, Billy feeling both apprehensive and excited about what was going to happen. Tendrils of steam floated in the air. A man took his buckets and filled one with hot water and the other with tepid. Adil led him into a third room, and as he entered it, Billy was smothered by what felt like a blanket of humid heat. He could just make out the figures of men sitting against the walls, dozing or chatting.

'Sit here,' said Adil. 'Now we must sweat.'

They sat in silence for a long time, Billy gradually succumbing to an easy torpor. Men came and went, their brown bodies looming in the milky light. Billy looked down at his own whiteness, and then he noticed that his sweat was dark with dirt.

'You Westerners never really get clean,' said Adil, 'for all the baths you take. You must sweat it out, it's the only way.'

Billy washed himself with the soap and water, and then a masseur came up and took hold of his arm. Leading him into yet another room, he sat him down and began to knead his shoulders and arms. Now and then Billy heard a loud cracking noise, and pain shot through him. The masseur smiled enigmatically, turning him this way and that, manipulating his limbs firmly. There was a physical intimacy to all of this that made Billy feel very uncomfortable.

The man lay on the floor, his knees arched, and motioned to Billy to lie on his back on top of him. Billy wondered what he was expected to do, but then the masseur grabbed him and draped his body across his own. The small of his back was now resting on the fulcrum of the masseur's knees. For a few moments he was terrified, convinced his back would break. The masseur held onto his arms, and Billy swayed in the air, willing it to end. When it did, the masseur stood up, took a bucket of water in his hand, and splashed it over him. It was icy cold, and shocked him into a new alertness. Adil appeared and said, 'You are now as clean as an Arab.'

As they walked towards the house, Billy felt a sense of physical exhilaration he hadn't known in a long time, his skin caressed by the warm evening air. He was almost dizzy with pleasure.

Adil's house was small and bare, and it was immediately clear that his family were poor. Billy was greeted by his mother, who wore a veil, and his sister, who was probably about eighteen and who revealed her pretty face. Adil and Billy sat down on cushions beside a low table, and Adil began to pour tea, tasting it and then returning it to the copper pot. He did this several times before deciding it was properly brewed and handing Billy a small tumbler. Adil's mother and sister stood above them, watching silently.

'Where is your father?' Billy asked.

'My father is sadly dead. He died of cancer two years ago.'

'I'm sorry.'

'I am the head of the family now.'

With this he nodded at the women, and they turned towards the kitchen. Billy looked around the room. The walls were roughly plastered and stained here and there. There was no decoration except for the rug on the floor and the red cloth that covered the table. Adil's sister brought in what looked liked tall earthenware hats, and Adil took away their lids to reveal dishes of beef and chicken and couscous.

'You must eat with your hand, with your right hand,' said Adil. 'Wait until it cools a little.'

Billy looked up at the women, who stood near the door, and wondered whether they would be eating with them. 'Will your mother and sister join us?' he said.

'They will eat later.'

The beef was stewed with prunes and the chicken with lemon, and they were both delicious. Billy observed how Adil ate, and did his best to follow, but made a dreadful mess nonetheless. After the meat came sweets, slabs of fudge and honey pastries, and then the women brought ewers of water and towels. Adil lay back against the wall and said, 'What do think of Marrakesh?'

'It's fascinating. I've never been anywhere other than England before. I can't really believe I'm here.'

'I've been to France, but never to England.'

'Were you studying there?'

'No, I just wanted to see where our masters came from.'

'They're not your masters now.'

'Perhaps not. But their trace remains.'

'Colonialism is over for all of us, surely?'

'Colonialism is a state of mind,' said Adil, 'no matter who might be occupying the barracks.' He sipped his tea. 'The French left us some things. But it was robbery nonetheless.'

'The British were worse, I'm sorry to say.'

'They were more successful, that was the only difference.

And more practical. The French had the idea they were civilizing us, bringing us the great gift of their culture. Still, they were not so cruel here as in Algeria.'

'So what now for Morocco?'

'What now? Modernization, of course. But we will never do more than scratch the surface. We are old here, very old.'

'I want to see something of the country,' said Billy. 'The mountains and the desert.'

'You will see how the Berbers live. We Arabs are colonizers too: this country is really theirs.'

'I've been reading about the Glaoui tribe. I want to go to their fortress.'

'It's abandoned now, and crumbling. But, yes, you must see it. Telouet, it's called. And then you can go to the desert.'

'I want to go as far as I can.'

'Then that is the edge of the desert, unless you are thinking of taking a camel train.'

———

He met Erin and Brad in the Café de France, and they sat drinking mint tea for a while before venturing into the Djemaa el Fna. At night the scene in the big square seemed almost apocalyptic, a confusion of noise, smoke, incense and light. Africans in white robes danced ecstatically to the sound of drums and castanets, the red tassels of their caps whirling in the air. The storytellers held their audiences spellbound, leaping from one spot to another within the tight circles of people, staring intently at them for greater effect. And the snake charmers played their lutes and cajoled rather than charmed the vipers and cobras into their lazy routines.

They strolled past the food stalls, gazing at the kebabs of meat and chicken and fish that lay ready for the brazier, and resisting the hustle of the touts. Eventually, and for no particular reason, they chose a stall and seated themselves on a bench. Tilley lamps hung above their heads, gathering smoke into their beams.

'The cheapest thing to have is a soup they call *harira*,' said Erin. 'It's kind of thick, with bits of lamb in it.'

'OK,' said Billy.

The waiter was clearly disappointed by the meagreness of their order, and pleaded with them to have some meat. Eventually he gave up, and tossed a basket of bread onto their table with an air of profound displeasure. Billy looked around him. The instruments of the various entertainers clashed with one another constantly, so that no single melody prevailed.

'Isn't this great?' said Brad.

'It's astonishing,' replied Billy.

'Just think, this must be what the place looked like a thousand years ago.'

Their soup arrived, and they picked up their spoons and began to eat. It was spicy and nourishing.

'So what have you seen so far?' Erin asked.

'Oh, not much in the way of the sights,' replied Billy. 'I've been soaking up the atmosphere.'

'You mean you haven't been to the Saadian Tombs, and places like that?'

'Not yet.'

'That's weird!'

'Do you think so?'

'Let's go there tomorrow. I want to see them again anyway. The Saadians were a dynasty of sultans, and their tombs were only rediscovered at the beginning of the century.'

'I know I *ought* to see these places...' said Billy.

'Let's do it, then.' Erin paused for a moment, laying down her spoon. Then she said, 'Hey, you know what? We're like Port and Kit and Tunner in *The Sheltering Sky*.'

'Oh, God!' said Brad. 'Does that mean I have to die horribly of fever?'

'And I have to have an affair with Billy.' She looked at him mischievously. 'Have you read it?' she asked.

'Yes,' he replied. 'Port dies, Kit goes crazy, and Tunner's left behind. And all because they wanted to see the desert.'

The air around them seemed newly charged, and not by the noise of the square. Billy was conscious that Erin looked at him now and then in a very candid sort of way. Had she meant anything by her remarks about the characters in the book? Suddenly he found himself weighing his words carefully.

'So where did you two meet?' he asked.

'At NYU,' replied Brad. 'We were both studying international relations.'

'And what do you plan on doing after the Peace Corps?'

'Oh, we're going to be in the State Department. We've already applied. And you?'

'I don't know. I'm not thinking beyond Morocco at the moment.'

'What did you do in England?'

'I dropped out of university and went to work in a bookshop in London.'

'You're going to turn that journal into a book, aren't you?' said Erin. 'You're going to be a famous travel writer.'

'Sure.' He smiled ironically. 'I'll send you a signed copy.'

———

Billy loved the city in the early morning, when the streets were watered and still gleamed in the sunlight, and the only other people up were the merchants and workers. He walked from the hostel to the Café de France, along the now-familiar alley. A man brushed past him carrying four chickens upside down. At first Billy thought they were dead, but then he realized they were alive but motionless, resigned to their fate. Cyclists weaved past him, tinkling their bells continually.

He sat at his favourite table in the café, ordered coffee and bread, and opened his journal. He had by now filled twenty pages with his impressions and thoughts. He had no idea whether he would ever attempt to put them into order, but for the moment he was content with these random jottings.

He saw a blonde woman heading across the square towards

him, and laid down his notebook. Erin was alone.

'Where's Brad?' he asked.

'He's sick. He reckons it was the harira, but I'm OK, and so, it seems, are you.'

'I'm sorry.'

'He gets sick easy. I worry about how he's going to be in Senegal.'

She joined him for a coffee, and they walked to the tombs. The street took them through a district of artisans, and everywhere men scurried about, wearing blue overalls and skullcaps and looking intent on their business. In a little workshop two of them inspected a piece of ancient machinery, divining its secrets and then bringing it suddenly to life.

They arrived at the entrance to the tombs, and saw that a queue had already formed.

'I hate seeing places with gaggles of tourists,' said Billy. 'Let's come back later.'

'Where shall we go now?' asked Erin.

'Let's go to the Aguedal Gardens. They're just south of here. I've wanted to go there for a while. Apparently there are wonderful views of the Atlas.'

Walking past the palace, they stepped through a tall gate and were presented with what appeared to be an endless vista of trees and paths. They strolled through orchards of figs and lemons, the paths bordered by shallow channels in which green-tinted water eddied about. Ahead of them, shrouded in haze, lay the Atlas Mountains. After a while they sat down on a tiled patio.

'That's where I'm going next,' said Billy, pointing to the mountains.

'When?'

'Tomorrow.'

'How will you get there?'

'There are buses that take you so far. And then you hitch.'

'They say hitching in Morocco is dangerous.'

'Do they? I can't imagine why. People are so friendly.'

'How far will you go?'

He raised his hand to shield his eyes. 'To the desert, I hope,' he said.

'And what are you going to find in the desert?'

'I've no idea, but I feel drawn to it.'

'Sounds kind of spiritual.'

'Is it? I'm the least spiritual person I know.'

'But you're a dreamer.'

'Perhaps.'

They sat listening to the babble of water in the channel below them. After a while Billy said, 'So what do you dream about?'

She thought for a moment. 'About doing something useful, I guess,' she said. 'Something that helps the world.'

'Is the world ready to be helped?'

'Of course. What do you think we'll be doing in Senegal?'

'I'm sorry.'

'What hope is there if we in the West don't help those less fortunate than ourselves?'

'I just wonder…' He fell silent.

'You just wonder what?' Erin asked.

He looked down at his scuffed shoes. 'I suppose I wonder whether it's really our responsibility,' he said. 'I'm not doubting your good intentions. But wouldn't it be better if Africa could solve its own problems?'

'Well it can't. And, anyway, we created them in the first place, by stealing their people and their resources.'

'So you're giving something back now?'

'Yes,' said Erin firmly. 'That's exactly what I'm doing.'

————

They met again in the early evening, and Brad was still ill.

'At this rate we're going to have to change our plans,' said Erin. 'He can't go to Senegal like this.'

'That's too bad.'

She looked out across the square. 'Let's go to Yacout for dinner,' she said.

'What's Yacout?'

'It's a palace restaurant, a little north from here, I think.'

'Sounds expensive.'

'It's on me. My old man's just sent me some funds.'

'Are you sure?'

'Yes. Let's go.'

They hailed a carriage, which took them to a part of the city Billy hadn't yet explored. A young man led them up some steps and to a table in the corner of a pillared room, where they sat side by side on a low banquette. The walls were faced with brightly coloured tiles and carved cedarwood, tall teapots and vases standing against them.

'Neat, huh?' said Erin.

'I feel like a sultan.'

'I think you'd make a very good sultan. I'd like to see you in some flowing robes.'

'Like Lawrence of Arabia.'

'Yeah. Maybe you should get an outfit for when you go south.'

'I'd be taken for a Berber.'

'Wouldn't that be fun?'

'Not if I can't speak a word of the language.'

A waiter brought tea, and told them what they would be eating. There was a lot, one course following another in rapid succession. The centrepiece was a *pastilla*, a pigeon pie, which the waiter was very proud of, but which Billy found far too sweet for his taste. A group of musicians sat cross-legged in the middle of the room, making lovely, melancholy music with a lute, a single-string fiddle and a drum.

As they ate and talked, Erin now and then placed her hand on his arm to accentuate something she was saying. His mind returned to what she had said about Kit and Tunner in Bowles's book. Was she being flirtatious? It was hard to tell. And was he attracted to her? That was hard to tell too. But when a woman was being attentive like this, it was easy to respond in kind.

'You're a loner, Billy,' she said during a lull in the music.

'I suppose I am.'

'Don't you want to be with people?'

'I *am* with people. I'm with you.'

'You know what I mean. You're not *with* me.'

Billy sipped the strong, gritty coffee that had been set in front of them.

'I did ask someone to come here with me, but she said no.'

'Ah, so you're not a monk after all.'

'No.'

'Why didn't she say yes?'

'Because there was someone else.'

She was gazing at him now, resting languidly against the cushions. 'There often is,' she said.

'I wouldn't know. The truth is I don't know much about women.'

'Men don't.'

'Do women know more about men?'

'Oh, sure,' she said.

Billy knew that some sort of line had now been crossed. He put down his cup and said, 'Perhaps we should be getting back. Brad will be wondering where we've got to.'

'Oh, Brad,' she said. 'He's such a kid.' She toyed with her bracelet. 'I guess I'm going to marry him, though.'

They stepped back into the street, and he said, 'Let's walk. Let's just see where we end up.'

They walked along ill-lit alleyways, Erin linking her arm in his, and before long Billy recognized the way.

'This is my place,' he said after a while.

'Can I come in?'

'I don't know. I suppose so.'

'You don't sound too sure.'

Before he could answer, Erin raised herself on her toes and kissed him.

'I have one night before the rest of my life begins,' she said.

'So do I.'

'What shall we do with it?'

'I think we should sleep.'

'I guessed you'd say that.'

He wrapped his arms around her. 'I hope things go well in Senegal,' he said.

'They will.' She nuzzled her face against his neck. 'And I hope you find what you're looking for in the desert.'

At the door of the hostel he turned to watch Erin's figure dwindling into the darkness. He thought of Rachel for a moment. Perhaps he just wasn't ready yet for women. Erin turned to wave, and he waved back. No, he wasn't ready yet.

———

Billy gave his duffel bag and sleeping bag to the driver, who threw them on to the roof of the bus. Then he got in, hauling himself past the other passengers, all of whom stared at him with open curiosity, and into a window seat at the back. An hour or so after they were due to leave, the driver gunned the engine and they set off. Black smoke from the exhaust blew through the open window as they pulled out into the road. They followed the ramparts of the old city for a while, the driver sweeping past the bicycles and carts and mobylettes, and soon they were on their way south. For a long time the country was flat and the road straight, lined with trees painted white at their bases. Then they came to the foothills, and to terraces of cactus and walnut trees.

Billy sat with his knees braced hard against the seat in front, gazing out of the window at the changing scenery. Soon they began to ascend into the mountains, the landscape becoming harsher as they rose. As the bus negotiated the winding road, he had glimpses back into the valley from which they had come, and of the snow-capped peaks where they were going. In Marrakesh he had felt he could almost reach out and touch these noble mountains. Now they were just the other side of a pane of glass. He smiled at his reflection in the window. He was on the road, he was doing what he had wanted to do for so long. He was a traveller.

From the mountain pass the bus began to descend again, and then turned sharply to the left onto a dirt track. It rattled and shook, and Billy hung on to his seat. Eventually they came to the village of Telouet, where Billy and most of the other passengers disembarked.

There was a little café at the roadside, and he ate some couscous and drank gallons of water. He asked the waiter where the

Glaoui fortress was. The man had only a few words of French, and he pointed vaguely east. Slinging his bag over his shoulder, Billy set off down the dusty road.

The fortress quickly came into view, a vast, brutish structure that dominated the valley. Billy arrived at its forecourt and looked up at the massive doors. There was no sign of life, so he knocked and waited. A few minutes later one of the doors was drawn back, and Billy was confronted by an African who seemed to be built on the same scale as the fortress.

'I'd like to look around, please,' he said.

The courtyard was full of piles of rubble, and had many doors leading off it. The African beckoned to Billy to follow him, and led him into a large reception room. The walls were lined with carved wood, of the kind Billy had seen in the *medersa* in Marrakesh, but like everything else in this place they were disintegrating. There were gaping holes through which Billy could see the countryside beyond.

'It was abandoned in nineteen fifty-six, when T'hami el Glaoui died,' said the African, 'and remains unfinished.'

They ascended some stairs to the roof, and from here Billy could see how the fortress had been constructed from stone as well as earth. But everything was crumbling. How quickly the great legacy of the Glaoui had been effaced.

'It is unsafe to go any further,' said the African. 'We must go back.'

A hawk flew above them, crying sharply.

'How do I get to Zagora from here?' Billy asked.

'You must go to Ouarzazate first. How far are you going?'

'To the dunes.'

'*Insha'Allah,*' he said gravely.

'*Insha'Allah?*'

'If God wills it.'

Billy looked up at the smooth, dark face of the African. There was a kind of serenity about him, the keeper of this ruined place.

'I hope He wills it,' he said.

The African bowed. '*Insha'Allah,*' he said again.

———

The owner of the café gave him a room for the night, and in the morning Billy caught a bus to Ouarzazate. Beyond the mountains the landscape changed again, rocky escarpments running alongside the road, their honey-yellow colour contrasting brilliantly with the blue of the sky. Ouarzazate was a dusty, shabby place, and he lost no time in getting on a bus to Zagora. By late afternoon he had crossed another high pass and was in the valley of the Draa River. Palm trees stretched into the distance, and at the roadside men and children stood holding out boxes of dates. This was Berber country now; the faces were nut-brown and weathered, the garments and headdresses gaudily coloured.

Like Ouarzazate, Zagora consisted of a single long street with houses on either side. Billy found a room, and in the evening went out for something to eat. He found a cheap café that was used by workmen, and sat beneath a faded portrait of the king, eating a meagre chicken tagine. He must be the only foreigner for miles around, he thought, and this made him feel oddly proud. His French was of little use by now, and he was more alone than ever. But this was a deeply satisfying sort of loneliness.

The nights were cool now and, having left his jacket in his duffel bag, he shivered as he walked back to the hostel. His room was a cell, with no electric light, and he read by candlelight for a while before turning in. He spent a restless night, images of the dunes coming always to his mind. He was so close now.

Not being sure of the buses from Zagora onwards, he walked to the end of the town and stuck out his thumb. Many who passed took this as a sign to honk their horns and cry out to him from their lorries and vans. A Peugeot estate car already containing five people pulled up, and the driver asked him in halting French where he was heading. Billy had read about these taxis that plied the roads, picking up and setting down people where they wished. He would have taken it if there had been anywhere to put his bags, but in the end he waved it on. Then after an hour or so a Bleriot lorry pulled up, and the driver said simply, 'Tagounite.'

Billy knew from the map that this was very near M'Hamid and the end of the made-up road, so he stowed his bags in the back of the lorry and opened the passenger door. With a grinding of gears they drove out of the town and towards the sun. The driver stroked his black beard and said in French, 'Tourist?'

'Traveller,' he replied, but it was clear that this distinction was lost.

The driver pointed at himself and said, 'Goats.' Billy turned to look through the rear window, and saw that the platform was covered in straw and littered with dung.

'Good,' he replied meaninglessly.

'Goats good.'

They drove on in silence, the road passing through a scrubby landscape that was not quite desert, an escarpment ahead of them clearly forming the last barrier before the dunes. After a couple of hours a divide in the hills began to appear, and they gained height again so as to pass through it. Billy drew in his breath, and very soon beheld a country of sand. Just a few miles away was the edge of the desert.

'Dunes,' he said, pointing.

'You go there?'

He nodded. They drove on for a while, the outlines of the desert becoming clearer all the time. Then Billy saw a wooden sign off to the left, which read simply 'To the dunes'.

'Stop here, please,' he shouted.

The driver put his foot on the brakes, and they came to rest.

'Thank you.'

The man looked at him with a blank expression, stroking his beard again. 'Money,' he said.

'Money? But I was hitching.'

He raised his hands in the air, clearly not understanding the word 'hitching'. 'Money,' he repeated.

Bill reached into his pocket and pulled out a tattered note. The man took it, and gestured with his fingers to indicate that it wasn't enough. Billy gave him another note, and then opened the door and retrieved his bags. The driver engaged gear and drove off. As the lorry disappeared from Billy's sight, he looked up and down the road, which was by now empty and silent. The sign to the dunes beckoned him, and he began to walk along the hard sandy track in the direction it indicated.

It was midday, and fiercely hot. In Marrakesh the October air had been kind, but here for the first time he felt the power of the sun. Having no hat, he shaded his eyes and gazed towards the dunes. Now that he was on foot he could see that they were nothing like as close as he had supposed. He thought about turning back, but pressed on. He was nearly there.

He walked all day, and into the cool of the evening. With the sun behind him he could make out the lines of the dunes quite clearly now, and could sense that he was making progress. Eventually the deep blue of evening gave way to the black of night, and he lay down by the side of the track, exhausted. The stars pulsed in the sky, brighter than he had ever seen them. Except for the occasional howl of a dog, there was utter silence. Billy ran sand through his fingers, sand that by now was quite cold.

Now that he was so close, all the reasons for his coming

here seemed to elude him. What was this crazy journey into nothingness all about? He recalled the things he had said to Tom and to Erin. How strange that such a strong determination had led him to this. What was it he wanted, really, from this barren place? What was it he lacked that the desert might supply? Tormented by doubts, he lay waiting for sleep to come.

He slept badly, the sand draining the warmth from his sleeping bag. Now and then he stood up and clapped himself with his arms, but when he lay down again the sand felt colder than snow. The night wore on, Billy dozing, turning on his side so as to keep his back as warm as he could. And then he was dreaming that his shoulder was being gently shaken. He opened his eyes, and in the starlight he saw three figures bending over him. He jumped to his feet, his heart pounding. One of the figures spoke quietly and soothingly, in a language he could tell was not Arabic, and which must be a Berber dialect. He smiled, and pointed into the distance. Billy resisted the urge to run away, and said in French, 'The dunes.'

The man repeated the word, clearly understanding it. He gestured to Billy to follow, and having no other idea in his head, Billy did so. They walked for about a mile, and then he saw a light. Soon they came upon a camp, three tents in a circle around a fire. One of the men called softly, and then there was an answering call. The man turned to Billy and made drinking and eating gestures. Now that he was no longer afraid, he realized he was weak with hunger.

They sat by the fire. A teapot hung from a wooden tripod, and a woman picked it up and poured mint tea into a cup, handing it to him. She went away and returned with bread and olives. Billy looked around him. In the firelight he could see that the tents were made of a dark sacking material, held up by wooden frames. The benches and the beds were covered with rugs and cushions, and pots and pans hung from struts above his head.

The woman was joined by another, and then by wide-eyed children. They watched Billy as he ate, encouraging him and smiling when he made a sign of satisfaction. He could now see the men's faces, and they were deeply lined, their eyes hooded and black. Billy made appreciative noises in French, knowing that the words would not be understood, but hoping that at least the sentiments might. He felt a strange mixture of exhaustion and exhilaration. That these people should have found him and taken him in like this seemed somehow miraculous.

After a while the man who had first shaken him awake took his hand and led him away from the tents. There was enough light now for Billy to see a herd of camels tethered nearby. The man spoke a command to one of them and it sat down, its front legs seeming to collapse under it, its hind legs following. Billy swung himself over the leather saddle and grabbed the boss with one hand and the reins with the other. The camel rose, hind legs first, pitching him forward and then back, and now he was astride it, high in the air. It made a sobbing sound, and flared its nostrils as though trying to identify this new passenger.

The other men mounted their camels, and one of them took Billy's reins, leading him on. The loping stride was more comfortable than he had imagined, and he held the boss of the saddle in a relaxed grip. Ahead of him the line of the dunes was clear in the pale light. The camel train speeded up, and now Billy tightened his grip. When they reached the edge of the dunes the softer sand slowed the camels down, and Billy found himself able to concentrate wholly on the scene. The ridges and hollows undulated far into the distance.

The leader dismounted, and Billy's camel went through the awkward movements of sitting down. Billy leaped onto the sand and raced up the slope of the dune. One of the men shouted at him, and gestured towards the ridge. There the sand was firmer, and Billy made better progress towards the summit. When he reached it, he could see an interminable expanse ahead of him. He sat down, looking at the place where the sun was about to rise. When it did so it changed the scene instantly, creating shadows that no sooner had they formed began to ebb away. A light wind was blowing, and Billy watched as the line of the ridge gradually shifted, grain by grain.

The sun blinded him now, shining, as it seemed, only for him. The Berbers had remained below, and he was sublimely alone. He sat enthralled by the strange world now wakening.

When the sun was up he stood and made to walk back down the ridge. Then suddenly he turned, and ran down the slope. His shoes filled with sand, and as they became heavier he lost his balance and tumbled forward. A cry of exultation broke from his lips. He picked himself up, smiled at the guides, and remounted his camel, turning towards the north. He had gone as far as he could go.